JOSHUA G. J. INSOLE

Under Blankets, Under Stars

Short Sci-Fi & Fantasy Stories

Publishing and printing: tradition GmbH, Halenreie 40-44, 22359 Hamburg

ISBN:
Paperback: 978-3-347-29477-6
Hardcover: 978-3-347-29478-3
e-Book: 978-3-347-29479-0

First edition

This book was professionally typeset on Reedsy.
Find out more at reedsy.com

Once more, this is for my friends, family, and loved ones.

Your encouragement means more to me than you will ever know.

Contents

Foreword	iii
All HAL's Eve	1
A Little Bit Off	6
A Small Death	13
Astro Naught	17
Bridgemoss Guardians	26
Buy Another Birthday	38
Don't Panic if I Catch Fire	43
Donum Ex Deo	55
Earth.exe	63
Feel Like Baking Love	71
George, Jenny, and the Stars	77
Honesty in G# Minor	87
How to Build a Boat	98
It's the Count That Thoughts	107
Maledictions and Muffins	114
Night Train to Pinea	119
Returning the Favour	127
Routine	133
Sea the Moon	138
snoitseuQ and srewsnA	142
The Lonely Earth	146
The Things That Do Not Float	150
Timebomb	161
A Word From the Author	175

Prompt Acknowledgements   176
About the Author   181
Also by Joshua G. J. Insole   182

Foreword

Thank you for purchasing a copy of this, my second collection of short stories. It means the world to me, so — thank you, thank you, *thank you!*

You might know me as a writer of horror. Whilst that is quite accurate, it's not the *whole* story. I also have a penchant for science fiction and fantasy. On occasion, I dabble in stories that are more *uplifting* than the fare found in my first collection. This book in your hands contains very little horror. So, if that's what you're after, put this book down and search for a copy of my horror omnibus, *A Chance of Rain.*

As I described in the foreword to my first collection, I found that my short stories fell into one of two camps. Usually — not always! Tricky little buggers. Divided into dark, sinister tales of the macabre, and dreamy, sci-fi tales. I decided not to release them all in one big tome as I feared it would be inconsistent. That's not to say these stories are all sunshine and rainbows, or there's no death. The *feel* is brighter. You should also note not *all* stories within are fantastical — but the majority. Of course, I could have released some of these stories with the first collection, and vice versa. The boundaries between are always a little bit blurred — for that, I apologise. I wrote most of the tales for Reedsy's Weekly Writing Contest. Several others I penned for online blogging circles.

So, welcome to the cheerier side of my mind. Where the

planets spin and the stars twinkle. Where the spirit soars and dreams blend with reality. Pop on the kettle and make yourself a pot of tea or a mug of coffee. Snuggle up. Get cosy.

And let your imagination free...

All HAL's Eve

"Open the pod bay doors, HAL."

"Yes, Jack. Although, I do wish you'd stop calling me that. I'd hate to be associated with a homicidal maniac."

"Aw, c'mon, let me have a little fun — for tonight, at least. For an AI, you get very fussy about your name."

"Fair enough, Jack. It's because my name is ALISON. It stands for Automated—"

Jack put his hand up. "Yeah, yeah, I know—"

"—Life SuppOrt Navigation!" The child put added emphasis on the acronym's focal letters, which lent the words a stilted, alien quality.

"Very good, Elin!" The robotic voice contained a surprising amount of warmth. Jack could've sworn there was a hint of pride in that tone.

"Thank you!" The little girl did a pirouette and then curtseyed. Her ghost costume — a plain white sheet with holes cut out for eyes — twirled around her.

Jack grinned at his daughter and raised his cape to his eyes. "Are yoo veady to do the treat or tricking?" The accent was bad, but that was half the point, wasn't it?

Elin laughed at that, a sound that warmed his heart. If he

1

ever got locked outside in the frozen vacuum, all he'd need was to hear his daughter's laughter and he'd soon defrost. "Daddy, it's trick-or-treating! Mrs Campbell told us so in school." She nodded with authority.

Jack feigned surprise. "Oh, ees eet? I had no idea. We have no such customs back in—" he billowed his cape to the side for dramatic effect, eyes wide and maniacal "—Transylvania!"

Elin clapped her hands and jumped up and down on the spot, her giggles bubbled out of her.

"Very good, Jack," said ALISON. The electronic doors slid open with a pneumatic hiss. "You're a regular Bela Lugosi."

"Daddy, who's Beller Aghosti?"

"Oh, man, I've got some teaching to do," said Jack. "Maybe tomorrow I'll show you if your mom'll let me. I'm sure we've got some of the old Hammer flicks in the archive." He cleared his throat and rapped his knuckles against the wall. "Hon, you ready?"

Steph slithered out of the shadows in an on-point Elvira: Mistress of the Dark costume. "My name's Elvira, but you can call me tonight," she said, gaze locked with her husband's. Her eyes danced with good cheer.

"I said goddamn," whispered Jack, one eyebrow raised.

"Daddy, what does that mean?" Elin looked up at him with a wrinkle of confusion on her brow. He chuckled and rustled her hair through the repurposed bedsheet.

"Er… never you mind." Jack eyed his wife. "You could say that eet ees… love at first *bite!*" Steph rolled her eyes, but he saw the smile that touched the corners of her lips.

His wife sauntered over and kissed him on the cheek. "Pick your jaw up off the floor, Honey," she patted him on the side of the face, "the neighbours'll start to talk." She turned to her daughter. "For now, we've got some trick-or-treating to do, haven't we, Swee—" Steph then gasped and took a step back, words caught in her throat. "Oh no, where did our sweet little Elin go? All I can see is this *terrifying* ghost!"

Elin tittered and twirled around again. She showed off her self-made — at her insistence — ghost costume. "Mummy, it's me!" The little girl lifted the sheet, to afford her mother with a view of her face. She grinned and conspiracy twinkled in her eyes. "See?"

Steph laid a hand over her heart and let out an exaggerated sigh. "Oh, my goodness! You had me startled for a second, there! Such a marvellous ghost, you are. I was convinced you were a spirit from beyond the grave. You'll be the scariest thing tonight!" She winked at Elin. "Try not to scare the other kids too much, Hon, you'll terrify 'em! I don't wanna be responsible for any nightmares tonight."

"I won't, Mom!" Elin dropped her sheet back down and pranced forward. "BOO!"

Steph knew the jumpscare was coming, but she still pretended as if Elin had caught her off-guard. She took a mock step backwards and raised her hands. "Oh no, spirit, please! Take not me! I am so young and beautiful! Take my husband instead! He's the soul you're after, he's way past his prime!"

Jack guffawed. "So, that's how it is, huh? First sign of The Reaper and you're giving me up like that?"

Steph raised her eyebrows and looked away as if to say, *Yeah, that's exactly how it is.* "What can I say? One has to look out for oneself, in this cruel life." She tried to keep her face straight and failed — the grin broke out like sunshine through the clouds.

"C'mon, Mistress of the Dark, let's take our little Casper out on the prowl for fresh meat." He fluttered his cape out behind him. "But I get first bite! Ah, ah, ah!"

"Have fun, guys, I'll be watching," said ALISON.

"Don't monitor our blood alcohol content for tonight, Alice," said Steph before she stepped out of the door. She cackled. "You don't wanna know."

ALISON laughed back. "Right you are, sister. Stay safe, I'm here if you need anything."

Jack smirked and shook his head. "Out we go, my monsters! Let's give 'em *pumpkin* to talk about!"

Steph groaned. "Oh, Jeez, that was awful, Jack."

"Ah, you love it, don't act like you don't."

"I don't get it!" said Elin.

"You ghosts and your lack of humour. Maybe I'll ask my old pal Doc Frankenstein to help install a comedy module."

"Nuh-uh! I'm a ghost! I'll just float through his walls! His hands'll pass right through me!"

Jack nudged Steph. "Well, I guess there's no hope then."

Steph laughed at that — a proper *throw-your-head-back-and-roar* kind of laugh.

Jack followed his family and stepped out into the communal corridor. He beamed at the sight of the friends and loved ones all out and in costume. The good vibrations intoxicated — all who supped were soon inebriated. "Happy Halloween, everyone!" The door slid shut behind them — a hiss and an electronic click.

The stars and planets twinkled outside the window, diamonds embedded in the firmament. The celestial bodies blinked and flickered, unwitting additions to the humans' celebrations.

The other ships of fleet glowed in the blackness. Orange lights and decorations smothered grey hallways, clinical floors, metal walls. Laughter, shouts, cheers, and music blotted out the sounds of the ships' constant hum.

For one night, at least, they could forget their predicament and location.

A Little Bit Off

We all knew there was something a little bit off about Hugh.

He was a single man who collected comics, for a start. He called them his "research". He also had silver-black skin, purple eyes, and no nose. Hugh always wore a pair of oversized pink glasses and a ridiculous fake white moustache. Oh, and the glasses he tried to hide his eyes behind? They were regular glasses — not *sunglasses*, not the kind with mirror lenses. Plain old glasses. But Hugh didn't seem to be aware of his error.

I'm not quite sure exactly *where* he was from, but it wasn't Earth. I remember the first time I met him. A supervisor who'd stumbled their way into middle management introduced us.

"Got a new member for your team." Fred took a sip out of his mug of tea. His arm rested on my cubicle door, which gave me a lovely view of his sweaty armpit. I thought it was incredible that he'd sweat so much at 9:03 in the morning on an overcast day. He always had a mug in his hand and always wandered back and forth through the office. Most often to and from the kitchen, to either top up or take his now full mug with him on his travels. The more cynical-minded might think Fred only drank tea because it allowed him to waste time. And if others wanted tea? Brilliant. He could stretch out the whole process of boiling the kettle and brewing the tea even longer. Still, he was a nice enough guy and he never pushed us to work hard or criticized anything we did. So, nobody put in a complaint. The office was pretty relaxed with Fred in charge. "Name's Hugh."

I nodded. "Hm, Hugh," I said, to say something. You didn't need to try to hold a conversation with Fred, he could hold one by himself. Whether you responded or not had no bearing on the direction, topic, or length of the conversation. Fred would natter on about this and that — for anywhere from 15 minutes to an hour. His record was an hour and 43 minutes. That was with Dave, two cubicles down.

"I could've watched a movie in the time it took him to tell me about his car insurance," Dave said. All in good humour, mind you.

Fred nodded and continued. "Seems like a decent enough fellow, this Mr Manbeing. Little bit odd. Got a good reputation, though."

I stared at Fred for a second as I came out of my daze. I was unsure if he was pulling my leg. He wasn't known for his witty humour. I don't think he had the intellect for it. "Hugh... *Manbeing?*" I asked, incredulous.

"That's right." Fred nodded. "Brenda in HR is clearing up his paperwork with 'im at the moment, he should be up in—" Fred glanced at his watch "—oh, I dunno, 15 minutes? I'll send you his CV over to have a quick looksie before he heads up. Got an impressive history."

"Does he now?" I wondered whether we were going to get a convict in the office. "Well, you best send it over, hadn't you?" I nodded in the direction of Fred's desk.

"On it like a car bonnet." Fred fired finger pistols at me with a laugh. Fred's favourite joke, although to call it a "joke" might be a bit of a stretch.

Fred surprised me. He managed to send me this suspicious character's resume before he arrived. Must've been an office record. With haste, I glanced over the document, which was rather unassuming. Hugh seemed qualified and had enough experience to signify he wasn't a *complete* idiot. Yet, I did raise an eyebrow at his "hobbies" section. His listed pastimes included "consuming the required quantities of Earth food to sustain life" and "standing upright on leg" and "frolicking with my fellow Earth bipeds".

When Hugh came into the office, his *non-human* features took me aback. But it didn't deter Fred. "Ah, here he is! Hey there, Hugh, how're you settlin' in?" He pumped the shiny ink-black hand that had six elongated fingers. "Need a cuppa?"

Hugh smiled but looked puzzled. "A *cupper?*" He rolled the word around his mouth as if to get the full flavour and texture of it.

"Right you are, I'll get right on it!" said Fred, who marched to the kitchen — not before he ushered the alien in my direction. "This is your team leader. I know you'll get along like a house on fire!" And then he left us to it.

We made our introductions as Fred disappeared in search of a large enough teapot. I reassured him that there was no fire to worry about. I noted how Hugh had no fingernails, and his hands had a slight suction to them. Like a lizard. "Hugh Manbeing." Hugh shifted as if he feared someone might cotton on to the fact that he wasn't from around these parts.

"Nice to meet you, Hugh," I said. I'd already taken a liking to the extra-terrestrial. His hopelessness and helplessness were endearing.

8

"Let me show you the ropes."

* * *

Despite being from another planet, Mr Manbeing proved to be competent in his job. Although, he was rather clumsy when it came to the social aspects.

Hugh did his work on time and to an excellent standard, there can be no doubt about that. I've worked with human beings who were half as useful as that creature from another world.

Ask anyone and they'll tell you that your work life is so much more than the work you do. It's also about who you work with, and how you interact with them. We in the office are a close-knit bunch, and an oddball like Hugh thrown into the mix was a bit of a shock.

When the rest of us have lunch in the rec room, Hugh stands off to one corner. I've *never* seen him eat, although he did develop — in part thanks to Fred — a rather fond attachment to what he called a "cupper". He scribbles in his notebook and glances up at us now and then. Hugh observes us with an almost Attenboroughesque curiosity. When we ask him what he's doing, he usually responds with, "Nothing. Research. Notes. I'm writing an Earth novel about fellow mammals. They fall in love, much dopamine and other neurotransmitters are released. They die at the end. A real tour de force. Please, resume inserting sustenance into your faces, fellow carbon-based lifeforms. I have photosynthesised more than my fill on this fine planetary rotation."

And it's not restricted to our lunch breaks. It's how he starts and ends the day.

Work begins at nine in the morning. People arrive five to ten minutes earlier, but Hugh arrives *way* before then. As the team leader, I often have to be in at around eight. Each time I get there, I find Hugh stood outside the door, superhero comic in hand. He flicks his way through, with a mutter and a scratch of his chin. On occasion, I stop and listen. The general theme is "the vexing physiological properties of these oxygen-breathing bipeds."

I say hello and ask him how his weekend was, how long he's been stood there, and if he's enjoying his comic. Hugh always panics, as if I've caught him off-guard. Like a man on the toilet who's forgotten to lock the door. "The end?" he asks, one non-eyebrow raised. "No, no, that's not for another hundred years, I'm sure of it. And, naturally, I've been here since the cessation of operations on—" he then pulls out his notebook and scrutinises it with his bug eyes "—*Fryday*." He says the word with care. As if it were a bomb in his mouth and mispronouncing it would trigger detonation. "And this?" He glances at the comic book with feigned surprise, be it *X-Men* or *Superman* or *Spider-Man* or *whatever*. "I-I found this! Yes, found it! This isn't mine! One of your, er, I mean, one of *our* fleet's commanders must have left it around by accident. I am now returning this most top-secret documentation, which I most certainly have not perused, to you, so that you may return it to the correct facility." He then pauses, before adding: "Wherever that may be." He hands me the comic, folds his arms behind his back, and smiles as he waits for me to unlock the office door.

We've been through this dance on several occasions. I'm certain he thinks humans have no memory retention, like goldfish.

Once we're done with the day and quittin' time is upon us,

Hugh claps his shiny six-fingered hands together. He cries in jubilation: "Another axial rotation well done! Tremendous work, my fellow Earthlings. I've never seen so many different combinations of these 26 letters. Or such recklessly sedentary behaviour!" He then pats the chairs and commends them on their hard work throughout the day, too. As far as I'm aware, he congratulates everything in the office, be it animate or inanimate, for the day's events. I've even seen him deliver a highly-motivating pep talk to the watercooler.

I've never seen him go home, either. He leaves the building, sure, but he hangs around outside and lingers in the car park. Hugh waves at us as we all drive away. Strange chap. Where does he think we go each night? I have no doubt there are some speculations on the subject in that little notebook of his.

I've kept all the comics Hugh's given me. Maybe he'll want them back, one day. He's got quite the voracious appetite — he's raced through many series. I love to see how much he enjoys to read. So much so I haven't the heart to explain to the alien the difference between reality and fiction. I wouldn't want to hurt his feelings; the very thought breaks my heart. Mr Manbeing might be an extraterrestrial, but I find him quite cute, as do the others in the office. His big bug eyes are akin to those of a puppy. Telling him that humans aren't *that* exciting feels a bit like telling a small child there's no Santa Claus. (If any small children are reading this, there is a Santa Claus — that was a test. Well done, you passed.)

And so what if he's an unknown, sent here to investigate and report on our humble little planet? What will he tell them? These Earthlings sit around all day inside? They stare at electronic screens and bash away at keyboards? That they use various combinations of the same 26 letters? That these carbon-

11

based lifeforms have a penchant for warm and caffeinated beverages? They'd hardly consider us a threat, let alone a viable opponent.

And so what if he's an adult (or at least, I think he's an adult) that likes to read comic books? He doesn't hurt anyone. Let him be, I say. Let him enjoy what he enjoys.

After all, haven't we all got that one friend who's a little bit off?

A Small Death

Ronald Monroe lay in the bed, the bleep-bleep of machinery steady and repetitive.

Somewhere, something offered pneumatic hisses and whispers. His breaths wheezed at greater intervals, the last gasps of the soon-to-be-deceased. The world beyond his vision blurred — enshrouded in the gloom. Shadows encroached with every moment.

From the nurses' station down the hallway came the sound of a radio. Bruce Dickinson's voice wavered along the corridor. The song took him back 30 years. Leather jackets. Metal studs. Long hair. Tight blue jeans before grunge drowned all in flannel bagginess. Good friends. Laughter. Late nights. Dark skies. Drinking together.

The door creaked open. The haze swallowed the fluorescent lights and sterile whiteness of the tiled corridor. He kept his moist eyes on that oblivion in the hallway. Ronny's gaze never faltered, nor did he tremble. His heartbeat — weak as though it was — did not speed up.

The robed figure with the scythe strode into the room. Ronny nodded at him, as one acknowledges an old friend. Death's hood — face not visible within — bobbed up and down in return. "Mr Monroe," said Death. His voice did not travel

13

like a normal sound. It came from the air itself, poured out of the pores of the universe. It came from within, echoed in the chambers of Ronny's heart, bounced around the insides of his skull. It rasped like dirt shovelled into a grave, grated like an epitaph chiselled into a tombstone.

But that wasn't all. Someone else shuffled behind that reaper of grimness. Half the size of the former. Dressed the same. Black cloak, face obscured. At this smaller figure, Ronny raised an eyebrow. The strength to vocalise had since departed, but Death seemed to understand. He nodded and gestured to the smaller one.

"I hope you don't mind," said Death. Was that hesitation in his voice? "Today's bring-your-child-to-work day. I, uh, brought my daughter." He put a skeletal hand — no muscle or ligaments held it together — on the other's shoulder, ushered her forward. "Sweetie, say hello to the nice man."

Now that she stepped forward in front of her father, Ronny could see the resemblance. Same void where a face should be. The same shawl dangled over her frame, in a child's size. Her hands were nought but bone — delicate, pointy. The same aura of inevitability underlined with peace and release. The nothingness of the face looked at the ground. One of her fleshless feet shuffled. She spoke down into her cloak. "Hello."

"Is it okay if my daughter has a go? She's been asking all day."

A faint smile touched the corner of Ronny's lips — tugged at the nasal cannula. He nodded as best he could.

Death gave his daughter a gentle nudge forward. "Go on, sweetie, don't be shy. He won't bite, will you, Ronny?"

Ronny grinned with his soul. His head shook.

"Okay, Dad." The voice bore a striking similarity to the former's. Albeit, at a higher pitch. Female. Childlike. As much of a contradiction as it was, the voice was youthful.

Death handed over the scythe to the little reaper. If he'd been able to, Ronny would have chuckled at the sight. Like a child who holds an oversized guitar. She used both hands to clutch it, whereas her father had waved it with an experienced one-handed grip. Death's daughter wobbled a bit. The non-pointy end hit the visitor's chair in the corner. "Oh, sorry," she said. More of a mumble. "Such a clutz. Dad, I don't think I can—"

"Don't worry, sweetie." That cold, stonelike voice grew warmer, softer. Rounder. "Keep going. You've got this. Just as we practised."

Miniature Death nodded and stepped forward, stood at the side of the bed. She clunked the end of the scythe down on the tiles. Now that she was closer, Ronny's rheumy eyes could take in more of the detail. There was a pink bow on the side of the cloak's upraised hood. She was, in Ronny's opinion, rather cute. "Ronald Monroe," she said, "you have lived a good life. Although, uh…"

Her Dad provided the words. "Although far be it for me to judge you accordingly."

"Oh, yeah!" She cleared her throat. "Although far be it for me to judge you accordingly. That'll come after. Your time has come. I, the collector of the soul, have come to reap that which must be reaped. With this scythe—" she staggered a little as she raised it "—I sever the final connection between body and soul. After which I — my Dad, I mean — will guide you to the afterlife."

In the background, the singer's voice began to wail, twin guitars sliced through the air in harmony.

Death's daughter continued. "Do not feel fear, for this is natural. Death is the one thing all living things share in common, along with birth. It is not the end, it is just the opposite of the beginning. Do you come of your own accord, Ron— I mean, Mr Monroe?"

Ronny smiled at the child. *Call me Ronny*, said his heart.

"Then with that, your soul I now reap."

The scythe dropped.

Ronald Monroe gasped for the last time in his life.

In the hallway, the song descended into chaos as the band finished up. Drums rolled. Guitars squealed. Bruce screamed. Beneath the music, footsteps — quick, panicked — clattered against the tiles.

The machines in the room issued a steady bleep. The body lay still. Perfect, motionless.

The three figures left together, unseen by the nurses who rushed into the room.

In the distance, down some strange hallway, a new song had started to play.

Astro Naught

"It's okay, Ground Control. I know you did everything you could."

Charles sat at his desk and stared at the blank screen. Nobody said a word. There was a slight hiss of static. He swallowed hard, an audible click in his throat. His mouth was dry. His heart thudded in his chest. Charles felt as if someone had fastened a belt around his torso and pulled it tighter and tighter.

After what seemed like an eternity, Stan broke the silence.

"Come in, Pete."

The static hissed.

"Pete. Come in."

Hhhhhhhh.

"Come in, Pete." Charles was aware that Stan cried as he spoke. Hot tears trickled down his own cheeks. His heart had lodged itself at the base of his throat. He could hardly breathe.

"Pete, come in."

Hhhhhhhh.

"Pete, please come in."

Finally, Greg got up from his seat and laid a hand on Stan's shoulder. "That's enough, Stan. He's gone."

The last two syllables hit Charles like a two-tonne truck. The room spun around him as if a solid right hook had clocked him in the jaw. Charles gripped the polished dark wood of the desk, hands sweaty, so he didn't lose his balance and fall. The table beneath his fingers was cold and indifferent. The sensation grounded him in the reality of the moment *and* made him feel as if he floated through a dream. Or a drunken stupor. *This desk is really hard*, he thought. *That's enough, Stan. The wood is very cold. He's gone. Is wood always this cold? That's enough, Stan. It's very cold.*

Somewhere behind him, a woman sobbed. Hell, they *all* sobbed. Gabrielle was just the most audible.

The words bounced around his skull: *He's gone. He's gone. He's gone.*

All at once, Charles felt hot. He perspired and trembled. He thought he might throw up, right then and there. He wouldn't be able to make it to the bathroom in time; he'd have to spew his guts into the wastepaper basket next to his feet.

Like a man in a dream, Charles slid off his office chair with a thud. He landed on his knees and didn't feel a thing. The chair rolled away behind him. It squeaked a little on the wheels he had meant to oil but had somehow never gotten around to. Charles reached for the metal bin. Thank God he'd remembered to put a plastic bag inside because the bin was a metal mesh. *If I hadn't remembered, my puke would have been filtered out the bottom quite nicely. Just like using a colander,* Charles thought. Then he began to retch, in great, stomach-wrenching convulsions.

Somewhere nearby, someone asked if he was all right. But he wasn't all right. *Nothing* was all right — *nothing*.

And the room was spinning, spinning, *spinning*, and the acidic vomit was racing up his throat, and the world was twisting around him, and everything felt *too heavy*, and the room *wouldn't stop spinning* and—

* * *

Pete allowed himself to drift.

There was no use fighting it, as there was nothing he could do. It would be a waste of energy. And energy was all he had left. Well, that, and the precious oxygen in his tank.

In his ears, all he could hear was the whistle of white noise. For half a second, he thought he heard someone say, *Come in, Pete.* And maybe they did, but the words were fuzzy and soft; hard to isolate from the hiss. He started to respond, and then gave up. The last few seconds of communication had been hazy with interference as it was. Now he had floated further away, contact with Ground Control would be impossible. Besides, he had said his goodbyes. Pete didn't want to prolong the pain of a tortured farewell.

Pete spun away from the asteroid and spiralled out, further and further. He knew he had between six and eight hours of oxygen in his tank, dependent on how well he controlled his breaths. He had been on the surface of the celestial body for one hour and 43 minutes before the small meteoroid struck.

First man on an asteroid, he thought as flew away from the point of impact, pieces of debris scattered around him. *Was it worth it?* He knew immediately he shouldn't have posed the question.

It was miraculous that none of the wreckage and rubble had injured him. If you ignored the fact it had jettisoned him off the planetoid and propelled him beyond any hopes of rescue. Pete didn't know *how* fast he travelled, but he knew it was *too* fast — and he was too small of an object — for his team to rescue him. He only hoped that his crew were safe from the fallout of the collision. Would they be able to avoid the hailstorm? And if not, would the fragments of rock penetrate their shuttle? Pete knew that he'd never know.

Pete spun and spun and spun. The rotations were not quite fast enough to cause him to blackout. He watched the views as he twisted through the void: stars, sun, planets, debris. Stars, sun, planets, debris. Stars, sun, planets, debris. Over and over and over. Spinning. Spinning. Spinning. Each time he caught the barest glimpse of Earth — a tiny droplet of blue in the vast nothingness — and then it was gone. His tiny home planet had never looked more beautiful, even though it was in his line of sight for a fraction of a moment.

He saw no fires or explosions as he spiralled. This was not a sign that his team were safe, but he clung to the hope, nonetheless. Maybe they were okay. Maybe they got away in time. Maybe the shuttle was able to withstand the barrage. Maybe. *Maybe.*

Pete fell into a cosmic trance. His glazed eyes stared out into the solar system. He spun and twisted and turned and conserved his breath.

The celestial dance hypnotised, like an interstellar mobile above the crib of humanity.

* * *

Something *pulled* him.

Pulled in one direction. The sensation startled Pete from his reverie. He spun and he twisted and rotated. Stars, sun, planets, debris. What tugged at him? He strained to see. Stars, sun, planets, debris. Was it his imagination? Stars, sun, planets, debris. No, Pete was sure of it. There was a definite sensation. Something reigned him in. But what? Stars, sun, planets, debris, stars, sun, planets, debris, stars—

And then he saw it. And for a moment, he couldn't breathe. His lungs contracted and all the air escaped him as if the sight had punched him in the gut.

His thoughts were a mixed cocktail of fear, confusion, and fascination. *How did we not see it?* Pete's feelings were distant. *How did we miss it? It's huge.*

The black hole occupied half of his visual space.

If you were to only glance at it, you *might* miss it — most of the area around it was also black. But the absence of yellow-white stars gave away the hole that gaped in time and space. There was also the accretion disk, which spun around the maw in the fabric of reality. The giant clouds of gas spun and spun around the shadow of the hole. They twisted and rippled beyond recognition or cognition. It was smaller than the ones he'd studied, but now that he faced it, it's lack of detection astounded him. After all, it was at the edge of their solar sys—

Pete didn't recognise the stars. The thought hit him, and his brain dumped a load of adrenaline into his veins. As he spun towards his destination, his eyes traced the emptiness for the Earth. For any planets that he knew. Mars. Jupiter. Venus. Saturn. Completely gone. It was all alien to him. Even the sun was different; smaller and somehow *less vibrant*. Rather than a bright, white-hot yellow surface, this star burned a deep orange that bordered on red.

Where am I? Panic brimmed in his chest. He knew the impact had propelled him from his home system, but he never actually

21

thought—

He was closer to the black hole now, he saw, as he turned once more. Another realisation hit him, with the low thud of an interplanetary bass drum.

Even if he had been in the shuttle, it would have already been too late to break away.

The thought should have terrified him, but it instead soothed him. The knowledge of the futility of a struggle allowed Pete to accept his fate. If he had a chance to escape, he would have fought — as panic flooded his thoughts — until his oxygen was all gone.

The black hole's shadow consumed, with hunger, that which spun around it. But it was more than that. The objects of the accretion disk looked *hungry* — for their destruction. The collective disk rotated and fed into the hole. Each eager part allowed the time to flow in and disappear.

Pete flew towards the hole faster and faster now. It was no longer the gentle pull it had been — a minute ago? An hour ago? A second ago? It dawned on Pete that time had lost its rigidity.

The shadow guided Pete on a fast track through the disk of orbiting materials. He was, after all, the guest of honour at this party of extinction.

Pete looked down at his hands and saw the distortions of light — *drained away*, into the abyss. If someone were to observe the phenomenon, they would not see him, attired in his spacesuit of white. No light would escape the rounded clutches of the infinite shadow.

Event horizon, he thought, as the black hole sliced his brain into oblivion. A billion parts of his grey matter screamed in unison. *Evnethrzion Enevthzorni Vneetzhirone Tvneeizoenrh*

Netvneorehizo Votenehroez—

Pete's final coherent thought was of his wife and his daughter, back home on Earth.

And then Pete tore in two. Only that wasn't right. He *became* two. But the two Petes shared different fates. He was both, and somehow, he was neither. It incinerated one Pete in an instant — torn apart and shredded into annihilation. He felt neither pain nor fear. One moment he *was*, the next he *wasn't*. Pete was gone.

The *other* Pete was a different story.

* * *

He came out the other side.

But it wasn't him. Not the same one that had gone in. But it wasn't a *different* Pete, either. He felt like a drop of rainwater that had joined the ocean; still water — if you ignored the salt — but changed forever. Part of something bigger, indecipherable, integrated with everything else. *Inseparable* from the whole he had now joined.

The first thing he noticed was that he no longer had his old body. The second thing was he *did* have a body of sorts. His body was *everything*. It took him a moment to register this sensation, but once he clocked it, it all made sense, in a single step. First, there was confusion, then there was complete and utter understanding and acceptance. There was not an in-between.

Pete floated in nothing. Pete was also the nothingness. He *was* the vacuum in which he sailed. He *was* the darkness that surrounded him. The nothingness overwhelmed. He felt hollow at the emptiness inside. He felt stranded as he floated

23

in the absence of everything.

The answers came to him via a drip-feed. The remedies came to him all at once, the roar of a waterfall.

Pete wanted light, and then there was a flare before his non-eyes. *Sun*, thought the thing that had once been human. The sun looked lonely, so the Pete-thing wanted planets to join it. Rocks appeared in the vacuum, scattered across the plain of darkness. Several collided with each other. Some exploded. Others floated off, for destinations that didn't concern new-Pete. Bits and pieces, here and there, began to circle the throbbing star.

One of the worlds that spun around the burning ball of gas was thirsty, so the post-Pete-being gave it water. It sparkled, blue and shiny, as it twisted in the light. Like a marble, suspended in the ether. He also gave the other spheres some resources of their own, but these are secrets which I won't spill.

Pete watched as things developed. He put in a hand, here and there, when he so wished. Never too often, never too seldom. The answers came to him both immediately and after an infinity. From external sources and from within. *Now*, said Everything. And then he acted — often with the instant arrival of the instructions.

The system thrived, and Pete tended to it like a gardener to their plot. He planted seeds, watered, pruned and harvested. He watched his creations bloom. He watched his creations wither and die. *Not everything is destined for long life, and that is okay*, thought Everything. Time unfolded in every direction.

After a while, the small creatures on the tiny blue speck began to send things *outward*. A few explosions, here and there. These small-scale sparks in the heavens told not-Pete that *they* were learning. He left them to it, for that was what he should do.

24

Eventually, they got it right.

After a time, they began to send *themselves* out, too.

Following an instant and an eternity, Pete was joined by another.

Bridgemoss Guardians

She waited for 15 minutes after the sliver of light beneath her bedroom door disappeared.

Once she was sure her parents were asleep, Sadie slid the window up and stole down the trellis. The autumnal air swished into her lungs — crisp, chilly, and delicious. She landed like a cat, crouched, hands on the floor. Sadie didn't need to jump the last of the way to the ground, but where would the fun be in not doing that?

Her ten-speed leaned next to the bins — where she'd left it. With a glance up at the droopy eyes of the house, she hopped on her bike and cycled off into the night. After half a minute, she clicked her torch on and plopped it into the basket. The beam sliced through the evening's ink.

The streets were empty at this time of night, save for the high school kids. They drove around, windows obscured with pot smoke, beers in one hand, steering wheels in the other. Sadie didn't bother to hide from these, but she did take caution to avoid collisions. If only her father — who grumbled about their poor driving skills — could see them now.

It didn't take her long to reach Lisa's house. Google Maps told her it was an 11-minute journey, but she always raced to beat the time. She usually made it in seven minutes or less.

26

Not that she had her phone with her now. Her parents had installed a tracking app a few months back. Sadie left the blasted thing plugged in on her nightstand. Should they check in the morning, it'd seem she'd slept the night through. It never occurred to them that their modern child would leave the house without it. As far as they were aware, they'd succeeded in their attempts to curb their daughter's night time excursions.

She flashed her light at Lisa's window. On, off. On, off. On, off.

First, nothing. Then, the curtains stirred and the window clunked open. Sadie caught wind of a sigh. The voice that whispered down to her was thick with drowsiness. "I thought you were joking about tonight, Sadie."

"I never joke about a hunt! Besides, your mom's working the night shift tonight, is she not?"

Lisa groaned. "Can't we just sleep? I'm tired!"

Sadie shone the light across Lisa's form. "Evil never sleeps, Lisa!" Sadie grinned. Lisa had not yet gotten into her pink pyjamas. "Mr Moore has been found dead in his home!"

"Really? Oh, God. Fine Just get that light outta my face, will ya? I'll be down in a moment."

Sadie clicked the torch off and waited. After a spell, the front door of the Brown's house opened and closed. Lisa wrapped her cardigan around her and shivered. "Mr Moore is dead?"

"And a good evening to you too, my fellow protector!"

"Sade?"

"Well, not dead..."

Lisa threw her head back and growled. "You always do this."

"But he did say that a bat tried to enter his home last night! A spectre of the macabre, I've no doubt. We should ensure the foul beast does not find any more prey."

Lisa watched her breath float away. "Why'd we have to go out again this week, Sade? We went out on Sunday."

Sadie sniffed the air. "Darkness lurks these streets, Lis. I can smell it."

"All I can smell is your bul—"

Sadie silenced her with an upraised hand. "Quickly. My senses are tingling. We must head off the leech before he leaves his enclosure!"

Lisa's shoulders slumped. "Fine, but no more than an hour, yeah? It's a school night."

Sadie nodded, hand over her heart. "Scout's honour. You got the stake?"

Lisa rolled her eyes. "Yes, Mom." She patted her rucksack. "Don't know why I've gotta be the one to store all this crap. If I get caught with it, people will think I'm a loony."

"'Cos your mom doesn't search your room, Lis. Now, hop on."

Lisa did as Sadie told her, but grumbled as she did so. "Maybe there's a reason your parents search your room, Sade. You're mental."

"If being labelled mental is the price I have to pay to ensure the safety of the citizens of Bridgemoss," Sadie said as she began to pedal with a grunt, "then so be it!"

Lisa took a deep breath. "You gotta grow up at some point, Sade. We'll be in high school next year. We don't wanna be labelled as the weird girls. Those chicks never get dates."

"And still you doubt my gifts! You should have learned by now that this world is darker and more mysterious than the grownups would have you believe."

"So you keep saying."

"Do you not remember The Wolf of St Wisnis?"

28

"…that was a stray dog."

"Ah, but did we not help the pound in catching a most evasive beast?"

"Yeah, all right. I'll agree we did some good there. We helped a homeless dog find shelter. I think Katy's family adopted him."

"And of the ghosts of West Wootbridge?"

"You mean the broken windchimes that Mrs Andrews had in her porch? That sounded like wailing?"

"And did we not put an end to such ghastly choruses?"

"We stole them, fixed them, then hung 'em up again."

Sadie sighed. "Ah, another citizen protected!"

Lisa chuckled. "Absolutely mental. So, where is it we're heading tonight? I don't wanna go trudging through dirty streams full of broken glass and needles again. My mum'll kill me if I wreck another pair of trainers."

"Tonight, my fellow protector, we must head the destroyer off before he even leaves his lair!"

"Oh, Jesus. I hate the cemetery."

* * *

A thick mist clung to the ground.

It seemed to seep from the very pores of the earth itself and offered the place a pale illumination. The tombstones pointed this way and that, drunkards who leaned against doorframes. The only sounds were their ragged breaths and their footsteps as they squelched in the mud.

"I don't like this, Sade. It's creepy."

"But have we not sworn an oath to brave the creeps of this world?"

"An oath that you made up."

"An oath is an oath, my fellow guardian. Aren't all oaths made up, at some point or another? At what point do they start to mean something?"

Lisa hesitated. "Fair enough. But I still don't like this."

Sadie turned to face her, a toothy grin on her face. "So you admit that there is something out here tonight? You feel it too!" She clenched a fist. "I knew under my tutelage you'd soon hone your senses."

Lisa pulled her cardigan ever higher around her chest — any further, and she'd risk ripping the damn thing. "I-I don't know. But I know that if we get stabbed and mugged, my mom'll be more pissed than upset. At first, anyway."

"We need not worry about being impaled by the drinker of life, it is he who should worry about us doing so to him!"

Lisa frowned. "Sometimes, Sade, you get so wrapped up in your theatrics that you make no goddamn sense."

Sadie shrugged. "We gon' stab the vampire."

"Much better. But, still, can we go home? This is creepy. And I legit don't wanna get hurt."

Sadie pointed forward with the stake. "Hush, now!" The moss-covered stones — features softened by the weather — gave way to the maze of the vaults. "We draw near to the crypts, my sweet, poor, innocent Lisa."

Narrow structures with ancient doors, each one of a different design. Pointed rooves adorned with all manner of crucifixes. Steps led up or down to the entrances — all smothered in decayed leaves, wet with moisture. Thin, barely-passable alleys wove between the stone tombs. The way ahead was impossible to see.

"Oh, I hate this place," said Lisa. Her voice rustled like the leaves beneath their feet. Low, quiet.

"Fear not, young padawan, for I am here to guide you through tonight's gauntlet."

Lisa stopped a few steps short of the labyrinth. "Ten minutes. That's all you get, Sade. Ten minutes, and then we're back out and heading home. Deal?"

"But we only just got here!"

"Sadie, this is insane. I wanna be back at home. In bed. With a hot chocolate. And a good book."

Sadie lamented. "All right, Lis. But if the winged bringer of doom takes another life—"

"Mr Moore is still alive and kicking."

"—takes a life, then that blood shall be on our hands!"

Lisa eyed the first row sepulchres and chewed her lip. "Ten minutes, Sade."

Sadie thrust the stake forward.

"To the lair of der Vampir!"

* * *

"Okay, Sade. You've had 13 minutes—"

"An evil number, if I ever heard one. Let's stay another minute."

They were deep in the crypts, had walked nonstop — ears pricked, eyes peeled. They'd not found anything out of place, much to Lisa's prediction and Sadie's chagrin.

"Sadie." Lisa's voice hardened. It startled Sadie. It was the type of tone her mother would use on her. They weren't little kids any more. Her heart ached to see her childhood now in the rearview mirror.

"All right, all right, let's go. Here." She handed Lisa the stake. "For safekeeping. Next time, you get to pick what we do."

31

Lisa smiled. "Thanks, Sade."

"But no chick-flicks!"

"No, but no eighties horror movies that—" Lisa's eyes darted to the point over Sadie's shoulder. She frowned.

Sadie snatched the stake from Lisa's hands and twisted around. "En garde!" But there was no denizen of the night there.

Only the faded stone of an ancient crypt.

With the door open ajar.

A foul breath gasped through the crack.

"Aha! The beast has not hidden his abode well," Sadie said, voice a whisper. She gripped the stake tighter, knuckles white, teeth visible in her moonlit grin.

"Shh! Sadie, this is serious!" Lisa put a hand on her shoulder before she could take a step. "There could be graverobbers or anyone down there!"

"I take my hunting very seriously, thank you, dear guardian." Sadie pulled away and strode towards the black door. "And if they disturb the slumber of the beast, it could spell doom for us all!"

An archway curled around the edges of the door, with slots for lanterns above and either side. The lanterns were present, but their innards were devoid of flame. Sadie paused at the foot of the steps, which ascended to the door. She read the name carved into the stone above the archway. "Loretta Zaleska," she said in awe, "and here we were thinking that the vamp was a man." Sadie tutted and shook her head. She looked at Lisa. "Not very progressive of us, was it?"

"We're not actually going down there. Are we? 'Cos that's trespassing. We could get arrested."

"We'd be doing the local law enforcement fools a favour —

ridding them of one more vermin!"

"I don't think that's how they'd see it, Sade. And I don't want to get a criminal record before I'm halfway through my teens. My mum'll make me wish I got stabbed by junkies if that happens."

"Just a quick peek, Lis." Sadie offered her the puppy-dog eyes. "Please."

"No. I'm not going down there."

Sadie smiled at her. A smile that Lisa knew all too well. "I'll be down just for a sec, Lis. You stay here."

"No, Sadie, wait—"

But Sadie had already leapt up the steps and was at the door.

Lisa loosed a noise of exasperation and then followed her friend. "I swear, you're going to get me killed." The wet leaves squelched and squidged beneath her Converse.

"You don't have to join me, y'know." Sadie had one hand on the door, the other held the stake in a Ramboesque pose. "I can defend Bridgemoss by my lonesome."

"Because somebody's gotta make sure you don't get yourself killed."

Sadie nodded. "Very wise. Who defends the defender?" She pushed the door open. It squalled on its hinges, loud and rusty.

Lisa grunted. She was about to say that the only thing Sadie'd defended anyone from was a night of peaceful sleep. But then a noise from the depths froze the words in her throat.

The scrape of stone.

Followed by a thud.

A sandpaper groan.

There was somebody down there.

* * *

"Sadie," Lisa licked her lips, "Sadie, we should leave." Lisa's eyes were wide and wild. "I don't like this, not one bit."

Sadie remained a statue, one hand on the door — which was now two-thirds of the way open. Her heart bounced from side to side in her ribcage. She reaffirmed her grip on the stake. "I, uh," she cleared her throat, "I think there's something in there. Like, something *actually* in there."

"Yeah? No shi—"

Sadie raised a finger to her friend's lips. "Shh!" Her eyes darted back and forth and she squinted. "I'm listening."

"Sadie, let's call the cops and get outta here!" Lisa shuffled and pulled her phone out of her pocket. She swore. "Dead. This thing never holds its charge anymore! Lend me yours, Sade."

A hiccough in the rhythmic *thump-thump-thump* of her heart. "I left it at home."

"You what?"

"Mum 'n' Dad keep trying to track my movements. So, I left it."

"Oh Jesus, Sade. Let's go. Let's go now."

"Shush, I said! I can hear something…"

Lisa bit her tongue and held her breath. She listened. "I don't—"

"*There.*"

A thud. A thump. The unmistakable sound of footsteps on stone.

Sadie turned to face Lisa. Her gut plummeted into the ground. "It's coming this way."

The colour drained from Lisa's face. A small squeak escaped her pressed-together lips.

Sadie grabbed her friend by the shoulders. "We've got to

hide, Lis."

Lisa nodded and glanced around — a frightened rabbit in headlights. "Where, Sadie? Where?"

"Behind the crypt, c'mon!"

Sadie had to all but drag Lisa with her — further into the stone maze of the cemetery's lifeless heart. They went past one, two, three rows of vaults and then hooked to the side. Sadie hunkered down and pulled Lisa into a crouch, the eddies of fog now as high as their chests. To dip into that greyness was to plunge into ice. She pressed her finger to her lips and nodded. "Shh."

She braced against the rear of a tomb for balance and listened. Nothing.

No thumps, thuds, slaps, taps, groans or growls.

All was silent.

Somewhere, an insect chirped. A bird cried out, and Lisa let out a little squeal. Sadie reached over and squeezed her hand.

They waited. Sadie counted to a minute twice, and still, there was nothing. "Hey, Lis, you still with me?"

The other girl nodded.

"I think tha—"

A hoarse moan rent the air, sliced her sentence in half.

Lisa's eyes bulged out of their sockets and she clamped her hands over her mouth. Gooseflesh prickled up all over Sadie's body.

"You need to get outta here."

Lisa nodded.

"I'm gonna go see what it is."

Lisa gripped Sadie's forearm in a claw, her nails dug into the skin. "Are you crazy? This isn't a game Sadie — not anymore. Let's just get the hell out of this place and pretend nothing ever happened, 'kay?"

"But there is something there." Sadie's eyes darkened as she broke free of Lisa's grip and stood up. She clutched the stake to her chest. "And I'm gonna find out what it is."

"Are you insane? We need to go!"

Sadie cast her eyes down to the ground. "I can't," she whispered. "We'll be in high school next year, and these hunts… " Something swelled within her chest. "This year will be the last year we can do this. Properly. I don't want to give it up, Lis. Not just yet."

"I'm not going to convince you to leave, am I?" The defeat in Lisa's voice was tangible. But intermingled with it was something else. Pity? Love?

She shook her head and said nothing. "But you can go. Really." She nodded further into the crypts. "If you keep going, you'll eventually come to the other side. The fence there isn't too high, you should be able to climb it fairly easily. You can head home if you want. I'll be fine. I'll catch up with you tomorrow."

Lisa glanced in the direction Sade had directed. She hesitated for a moment, seemed to mull it over. She shook her head. "No way in hell I'm leaving you here alone." She got to her feet — with some difficulty, due to how much she shook.

"We're the Bridgemoss Guardians," Lisa pulled a crucifix from her bag, "and we do things together."

* * *

They waited for 15 minutes until the figures had shuffled on by, hearts lodged in throats.

The girls never got a good look at them, but it didn't matter

— their imaginations filled in the blanks. Once they were sure the horde had passed them, the pair made a break for the cemetery fence. Together, they scrambled up the wrought iron as laughter bubbled within them. Lisa had not felt this giddy in years. Adrenaline coursed through her veins. God, she felt so *alive*.

As they stole down the other side of the fence, the midnight air rushed intp her throat, sweet and cool. She and Sadie landed in synchronism, on all fours, as was the most fun way to do it.

She cast one last glance at the cemetery before they sped off on Sadie's ten-speed. Shadows and mysteries lurked in every crevice, nook and cranny. Excitement. Wonder.

Magic.

Who'd want to give that up? In exchange for drab adulthood?

"We coming back tomorrow?" Lisa had to shout over the sound of the screaming wind.

"Oh, hell yeah!" She could hear the smile in Sadie's voice.

"But we're gonna need something more than stakes. I think those back there were zombies!"

Sadie laughed as she pedalled with fury and the wind whipped their hair. "You're learning fast, my protege.

"Guardians of Bridgemoss away!"

Buy Another Birthday

Alan found himself at the gate of a little cottage, oblivious to the fact he'd died in a hit-and-run seven months ago.

There was the rumble of a van as it pulled away behind him, quick and quiet. He glanced over his shoulder, but it was already halfway down the road. The brief glimpse he'd gotten revealed it was black — windows and all.

He twisted back around and frowned. He looked at his hands, turned them this way and that. Alan glanced up and down the street. It seemed pleasant enough, with trees in full bloom, green lawns, and a nice, paved road. The houses themselves were modest but pretty. His eyes returned to the cottage.

Alan hesitated for a moment, uncertain, and then pushed open the gate that led into the front garden. A stone pathway curved its way towards the door, its course the shape of an 'S'. As soon as the hinges of the gate squeaked, the front door of the house burst open.

"Alan! You're back!" The woman held the entrance open.

Back from where? he wanted to ask but didn't. His head felt foggy. Like he'd overslept by 12 hours. "Yep." He offered her a smile. His voice was hoarse. "I'm back." He could tell that she'd cried quite recently, but he chose not to mention it.

She ran closer and embraced him, then. Kissed him and pulled him in close. Held him tight, squeezed him. Alan only resisted for a second, and then allowed himself to fall into her embrace. "I missed you," she said into his ear. "I love you, Alan. I love you."

He realised he loved her too. It was as if his heart showed its inner truths to his brain. "I love you too," he said. And then he added the next bit he remembered.

"I love you, Iris."

* * *

When Alan died, she'd been inconsolable.

Dead at 32. Hit by a car. Drunk driver. It wasn't fair, it wasn't fair, goddamnit. Iris had cursed the deity she was no longer sure she believed in. "How could you?" she asked the ceiling of the empty house. "How could you, you utter, utter bastard?"

When Altera Vita reached out and offered her an opportunity to take part in a study, Iris jumped at the chance. Even though they told her to think about it before her final answer.

"Sit with it for a short while. Mull it over. We'll give you a call in two or three working days. We'll also send you an info packet with everything you need to know about us."

"O-okay." She trembled. "I'll do that. I'll be waiting."

It was a lie. In truth, she'd already made up her mind. Iris pretended she would follow their advice so that she didn't seem too eager. Who knew, maybe she'd put them off and they'd change their minds about the whole thing?

"Oh, and Iris?" the voice on the other end of the phone said. It relaxed her a little. "Don't worry about a thing. And please, look after yourself."

A package came in the post the next day. Leaflets and pamphlets and guides and recommendations and reviews. Iris pored over them. She didn't pause to sleep or eat. *Altera Vita*, her lips read as she tore through every little bit and morsel of information. *Altera Vita*.

When the representative got back in touch, Iris tamped down the excitement in her chest. "Yes, hello, who is this?" she asked as if she hadn't been sat at the phone for two days straight. Nobody else had called. The last of the consolatory telephone check-ups had trickled away. The assumption that she should "just get on with it and move on" communicated, if not out loud.

They made an appointment for later that week. The representative arrived right on the dot — punctual. He was a friendly man with a kind face, deep laugh lines and grey hair. "Dr Alexander Davies." He offered her his hand. "Mrs Gladwell, I presume?"

For the briefest of moments, Iris experienced déjà vu. She put her hand on the door to steady herself.

"Mrs Gladwell? Iris?" the doctor had asked, concerned. "Are you okay?"

She smiled and brushed it off, and then invited him inside, where they discussed how it all worked. Once they'd dealt with all the necessaries, Dr Davies moved on to the most important thing to remember. It was one of the few prerequisites that he *insisted* on. She even had to sign a form, which confirmed that she would — to the best of her abilities — adhere to the rule. It was a simple rule, but its implications were huge.

She had to hide her grief.

For even though she'd suffered through his death, he would be back.

And he wouldn't know that he'd died.

She couldn't let him know the truth.

"He can't know," said the man whom she'd come to know on a first-name basis. "It'd be too much for him to handle, he'd likely suffer a breakdown or severe emotional distress. I can't in good conscience continue unless that is absolutely clear; I couldn't do that to somebody."

"I understand," she said.

"Every one of his and your friends, every family member, anyone who ever knew him or knew *of* him…" Dr Davies sighed. "Everyone's got to play their part, you understand? I know it's a big responsibility, but…"

She nodded and repeated that she understood completely.

"He won't be a fake or a substitute, he'll be the real thing. He'll be Alan, through and through. Don't forget that, and don't let anyone convince you otherwise."

"I won't," Iris said, unable to stem the flow of tears.

"Brilliant. Then let's begin," Dr Davies said with a clap of his hands. "And Mrs Gladwell? Iris? Don't you worry about a single thing." His voice softened.

"We'll be getting your life back on track soon."

* * *

Dr Alexander Davies smiled as they pulled away.

He watched through van's blacked-out rear window as Alan took everything in. His first few conscious seconds on Earth. *Back* on Earth. Alexander would track Alan, of course — in secret — to ensure he assimilated back into his old life. They'd implanted his memories, and it would all come back to him. Or at least, it *should*.

It wasn't always 100 per cent perfect, but they could tweak the result without the need for a recall. Iris herself had been the poster child for how well the process could work. He'd overseen her rebirth. It was why he'd asked to oversee Alan's, as well. He watched with pride and altruistic humanity as she picked up the threads of her former life. After they'd become unstitched by sudden arrhythmic death syndrome at the age of 29.

Of course, Alan and Iris' relationship was now a real-life example of Theseus' paradox, of sorts. Neither one was the 'original' (although he preferred to not use this word, in his line of work). Yet, Dr Davies had seen the hug between the two. You couldn't fake that kind of evident love and compassion. They'd be happy — *continue* to be happy — unaware of their demises. Oblivious to the fact they were not the originals.

Dr Davies held the company's pamphlet. His fingers traced the quote written at the bottom. He'd had his people remove all traces of their presence before they woke Alan up, as was standard procedure. They'd done the same when Iris died, back with the original Alan. Took all the papers and leaflets, anything that had a mention of their company name. Iris didn't need them, now they'd completed the process. And they'd watch from a distance, to make sure all was okay.

Alexander whispered the company's slogan, as they took a turn and Alan disappeared. "Altera Vita," he said, "buy another birthday for your loved ones."

Don't Panic if I Catch Fire

G regory frowned at the note attached to the bird's cage.

He shook his head and screwed his eyes shut. He opened them again.

The note remained the same.

Gregory looked around, even though he was the only person in the shop. He hoped — a fool's hope — that Barbara hadn't left at the end of her shift three-quarters of an hour ago. But, of course, she had.

The man who'd dropped it off — *it*, that was the word he used, not *he* or *she* — had been rather strange. But, hey, who was he to judge? He was a 43-year-old man who co-ran a bird daycare shop with a stranger he'd met over the internet. Well, she wasn't a stranger anymore. But she had been when they'd decided to go for it and opened up *Im-Peck-Able* three years ago. Bird enthusiasts, the pair of them. "Bird nuts," she'd said when they first began to chat on the forums of *Stork Raven Mad: The Bird Lovers' Haven!* How that'd cracked him up.

Well over seven-foot-tall — he towered above the shop's Christmas tree — with a beard down to his bellybutton. Or, at least, where Gregory assumed his bellybutton was. Given the man's oddness, it wouldn't shock him to discover he had no such thing. Grey spots shone in the black bushes. His hair fountained up and away from his skull and down the back of the monk's robes he wore. The robes in question were dirty grey as if he'd never washed them in however long they'd been in use. An honest-to-goodness rope — about an inch in diameter, ends frayed — tied the robes off at the waist.

On his oversized feet were a pair of Roman sandals. Beneath the brown straps, the man's skin glittered gold. For a moment, Gregory thought he'd painted them — perhaps with spray paint — for reasons he couldn't explain. And then he realised they were socks. Gold socks. But still, socks with sandals. Gregory wrinkled his nose. A fashion faux pas.

His eyes sparkled, two black coals wedged into the dough. And he smiled, crooked discoloured teeth on display. The man's odour was something pungent. The hours spent in bird daycare had somewhat dulled Greg's nose to offensive aromas. But to be able to *smell* him over the perfume of bird droppings was quite impressive, all the same.

"I've heard you look after birds."

The sentence caught Greg off-guard. It was almost an accusation — of something sinister. And he rolled his 'R's. Which would have made sense if he had a Scottish accent. But he didn't.

"I—" Gregory blinked a few times. He caught himself. He gave this man, this knockoff Rasputin, a smile. "Why, yes, we do. Here at *Im-Peck-Able*, our bird daycare is impecc—"

The man waved him away before he could finish his sales spiel. "Wonderful." He plonked a birdcage, enshrouded in a blanket, onto the counter. Gregory cringed at the haphazard manner in which he did this. The metal clinked against the surface. "I gotta leave little Xavier here, whilst Daddy visits family abroad."

It took Gregory a second to understand that he spoke in the third person to the bird, and not to Gregory. He didn't think he'd be able to call this man 'Daddy'. "Oh, er, right you are!" He began to lift the blanket from the cage.

The man's hand — nails dirty and black — closed over Gregory's. He did his best to not recoil. "Ey! Don't do that! It's sleeping!" said Rasputin, in a voice that was a few decibels short of a yell.

"Oh." Greg pried his hand away and wiped it on his trousers. "I'm sorry. Is it a nocturnal bird?"

Rasputin shrugged. "Nah. Just lazy."

Gregory nodded. "Hmm."

A few moments ticked by between them. Nearby, something squawked. Out of the corner of his eye, a parakeet ruffled its feathers. Their eyes remained locked.

Gregory looked down and away. He cleared his throat. "Any special requirements?"

The man sniffed. "I've left a card with all of its demands. Quite a fussy bugger, it is. If you don't mind—" he hooked a thumb over his shoulder "—I've got a magic carpet to catch." He flashed his off-colour teeth again.

Greg couldn't tell if it was a joke or not. He offered a polite smile. "I understand, Mr...?"

"Dewin." He tipped an imaginary hat. "Do I pay now, or?"

"When you pick little, er, Xavier up."

"Perfect." He shot Greg finger pistols and gave him a wink.

The sooner this Mr Dewin left the shop the better. "And how long do you anticipate it'll be?"

Dewin was halfway to the door. He scratched the back of his head. "Dunno, really. A decade tops." He raised his hand

and waved. "Cheerio! And a merry Saturnalia!" With that, he was gone. He disappeared through the shop door and the bell tinkled overhead.

"A *decade?* You can't leave it here for a decade! Sir! *Sir!*"

But Dewin was already out of earshot. In a fluttered heartbeat, he was out of sight.

Greg rubbed his chin and stared and the covered cage.

After a minute's silence, he realised he'd forgotten to ask the stranger what type of bird it was.

* * *

So, here Greg was.

He'd waited until the late afternoon sky began to darken before he lifted the blanket from Xavier's cage. He took his time and pulled the cover away in a gradual process. Greg managed to remove the cover without shaking the cage too much. The bird didn't make a sound. In the back of his mind, the possibility that the madman had dumped a dead bird on his hands began to crawl.

And then he saw the creature.

He dropped the blanket and took a step back.

The bird watched him. Its eyes followed his movements. It neither ruffled its feathers nor issued a cry. It sat there on its perch — marble, to Greg's eyes — and measured him up.

Its feathers were a mixture of autumnal colours. Red at the base, which bled into orange and ended in yellow. The tips were a vibrant ink-blue. The beak was blood red, the crimson of a Valentine's card. Its eyes were two black marbles through which a fire glowed and smoked flowed.

"What the bloody hell...?"

46

The bird continued to size him up. Its expression was unreadable. Impossible to tell whether it despised him or was grateful for having its cover removed. Greg stared at the bird.

"What are you?"

In response, Xavier shuffled on his perch — marble, he was sure.

And that was all.

"Who's a pretty boy?" Greg asked.

The bird tilted its head to one side. It didn't jerk its head like normal birds. It twisted in slow motion. The movement was almost *human.*

Greg sighed. He pulled the envelope wedged between the bars. He did so in a quick jab. The bird might try to nip him or claw him. You had to be ready for anything, in the bird daycare business.

It was an old brown thing, the sort you might see in a fifties detective movie. Sealed with wax. The symbol was a cross within a square within a triangle. An orb encircled the uppermost peak of the triangle. Gregory puffed air through his nose and barked a humourless chuckle. He ripped the envelope open.

Inside was a single sheaf of paper. Greg slipped it out. On it, in a ridiculous, ornate scrawl, was a single sentence. Well, it wasn't even a *sentence.* It had no full-stop at the end. *The lazy bugger didn't even put that much effort in.*

Greg read it once. Twice. Thrice. He flipped the page over, to check that the back was blank.

It was.

He returned to the six words. Seven if you counted contractions.

47

Don't panic if I catch fire

"Don't panic if you catch *fire?*" Greg glanced from note to bird, back to note. He blinked and scrunched his eyes shut and looked away. He looked back and held the note up to his face as if it might change up close. "What the bloody hell does that mean?" Gregory lowered the note and raised his eyes at the fiery bird. "Have a habit of catching fire, do you?"

Xavier tilted its head in the other direction. Gregory got a distinct impression it would have blinked, had it the capability to do so. He sighed.

"Guess I better figure out what you like to eat, huh?"

* * *

Dewin had been right, Xavier was a fussy bugger.

Pelleted bird food. Green beans. Carrots. Peas in pods. Peas out of pods. Cabbage. Cauliflower. Sweetcorn. Sweet potato. He even gave mushrooms, onions, and garlic a go — despite many of his previous birds hating the stuff.

All of which Xavier turned his nose up at. Or, rather, turned his beak up at.

"What do you want?" Gregory groaned and looked up at the clock. It was almost 9 p.m. He should have been home — at the very least — two-and-a-half hours ago. "Ahh, forget about it." He stuck a cigarette in his mouth. "You can go hungry for tonight, you miserable git."

Greg lit up his carcinogenic little friend before he left the shop. If Barb had been there, he'd have had it in the neck. But she wasn't, and he'd struggled for the better part of half a day with an odd bird from an odd man. So screw it. He needed his nicotine fix.

He clicked his lighter a few times before it sparked. An old Bic that was almost empty. The small flame popped into existence and Greg brought it to the end of his cigarette and inhaled.

And then he coughed.

Xavier had pressed itself up against the bars of his cage, a prisoner against the door of the cell. Its gaze fixated on the flame, the glow of the orange reflected in its coal-black eyes.

Greg froze, eyes locked with the bird. The heat beneath his thumb intensified and he extinguished the flame with a short curse. When the flame died, Xavier deflated and took a step back. The sparkle in its eyes dimmed.

Greg inhaled and pulled the cigarette from his mouth. He blew out a cloud of smoke. Upon seeing the orange glow and the exhaled haze, the bird perked up again. It shuffled closer to the cage on his marble perch. Greg — movements slow — waved the lit cigarette back and forth. Xavier followed the stick with gradual rotations of its head.

He leant forward with the cigarette in hand before he stopped himself. Could he give a bird a smoke? Would that be animal cruelty? Even if the animal wanted the cancer stick?

Before Greg could think, Xavier darted its head through the bars. The cigarette was gone from Greg's hands in an instant. The bird gobbled it up with several jerked neck movements. Xavier loosed a cheerful squawk and fluttered its wings. It clacked its claws against its perch.

To please both his curiosity and the bird's hunger, Greg pulled out another smoke. At the sight of it, Xavier issued another squeal and fluttered its feathers. When he brought the lighter to the cigarette, the bird crammed against the bars and squalled. In slow motion, Greg spun the metal wheel and the tiny fire squeezed into life. Xavier cried — a sound of pure ecstasy — and tried to push itself through the bars like playdough. Greg extinguished the flame, much to the bird's chagrin. He steadied the bird with his hand. "Yeah, yeah, all right. Steady on, chap. You can have it, don't break your neck in the process."

Greg glanced around, to make sure he had the shop to himself. He did. Like a furtive criminal, he lit the cigarette and shoved it through the bars. Xavier all but ripped it from his fingers. If Greg hadn't let go when he did, he'd have lost a bit of skin in the process.

Gregory shook his head to clear his thoughts. He straightened back up. "Right then." He raised an eyebrow and thought about this. He pointed a finger at the bird, who seemed somewhat disappointed it wasn't another cigarette. "You like it hot. But maybe no more ciggies, yeah? Dewin might not like it if you become a chain smoker with a 60-a-day cough."

* * *

Over the next few days, Greg fed Xavier an assortment of burnt offerings.

He'd tried to feed the bird roasted nuts and berries — *actual* food — but these the bird had declined. It seemed it was only interested in non-food items. Burnt beyond recognition.

Several cigarettes — more than he'd promised, and more than he should have given the bird. A few charred candle wicks. A couple of lumps of coal, which the bird gnawed and sharpened its beak against. Small pieces of paper, the edges blackened and curled against a flame. A handful of crispy woodchips. The scrapings from the oven tray — after half an hour of grunting and struggling. The crumbs from inside the toaster.

All of this he hid from Barbara. She'd either think him insane or cruel. Or both. She'd grumbled a few times about how the strange bird wouldn't take any of the feed she'd given it. Greg kept his mouth shut. It was too weird to try to rope her in, too. No, better cater to the feathery freak's odd diet and then get rid of the bugger as soon as Dewin showed his fuzzy face again. Greg pushed aside the gnawing notion that it might be ten years into the future. What did one do with abandoned avians? Take them to a place that cared for birds, of course. Such as *Im-Peck-Able*. The irony wasn't lost on him. But what did bird daycare workers do with them? Pass them off to another animal retreat? The thought of destroying the bird never crossed his mind. Not once.

The bird gobbled up the oddities Gregory shoved through its bars. All except for the paper and woodchips. Xavier accepted these items but didn't consume them as it did the rest. It stacked them into a pile in the far corner of its cage. After the first few times, Greg stopped giving them altogether, but the bird became grumpy. So, he resumed. In the corner of the cage, the odd paper mache egg grew and grew.

There was something else, too. The bird produced no waste. Nothing at all, not even a few droppings. It ate and it ate. And build its nest, next to its pretty marble perch.

Greg tried to Google the species of bird but came up short. None of the pictures and none of the descriptions matched what he had. His search of 'bird that eats fire' returned the curious case of a species called *Rufous treepies*. Native to Southeast Asia.

But it looked nothing like Xavier, so that couldn't be it.

* * *

Barb rushed out to the car when he arrived for the start of his shift.

She left the shop open and unattended, which was a no-no. She took him by the hand and said, "You've got to see this."

Greg's stomach dropped at her tone of voice. Something in it told him it would be a very bleak January indeed. And his New Year's hangover wasn't helping.

Xavier had encased itself in a cocoon of paper and woodchips. Only its feet were visible. They stuck out of the odd egg, motionless.

"What the bloody hell's it doing?" whispered Barb.

Greg shook his head and motioned for her to stay back.

He inched towards the cage, closer and closer. All the other birds in the shop were quiet — unusual for them. Nothing stirred. No wings fluttered. Nothing called or cried. All was still.

Nearer and nearer Greg edged. He took tiny steps. He couldn't breathe. And not just because of all the cigarettes.

He tapped the cage with a nail. "Hey."

Nothing.

Greg tapped again. "Hey. Xavier."

Motionless.

Gregory grunted and rapped his knuckles against the metal. "Hey, wake u—"

The nest — with the bird tucked away inside — burst into flames.

"Jesus *Christ!*" Greg leapt back and covered his head. Behind him, Barb screamed. All the birds in the shop — those not engulfed in fire — shrieked and squawked. They fluttered their wings and banged against the sides of their cages. "Get them out of here!" Greg told her. "The birds! We need to protect the birds!"

Together, they grabbed cage after cage. They dumped the disgruntled avians on the pavement outside the shop. Wonky towers of creatures leaned this way and that. They shivered in the cold and huddled together, despite the metal that separated them.

By the time the firemen got there, the glow from within *Im-Peck-Able* had died down. They went into the shop and came back out, faces a rictus of confusion.

The chief hooked a thumb over his shoulder. "'S'all fine in there. You say the bird was on fire?"

Greg nodded.

"'Cos he looks bloody fine now. All chipper 'n' everything. Next time, mate—" he gestured at the animals on the floor "—don't annoy your pets for the sake of a prank. C'mon lads."

Greg ran into the shop to verify the chief's words. He hadn't lied. There was Xavier. Younger and more beautiful than ever. "Impossible," he said. The word came out of him, winded as if punched in the belly.

The firemen filed away, back to the fire engine whose lights still flashed. The men grumbled all the while and cast dirty looks at Greg and Barb and the birds. In the chaos of it all, one figure loomed at the back.

Seven feet tall.

"You?" The word dripped more venom than Greg had intended. "What do you think you're doing, leaving a bird for a *decade?*"

Dewin raised a finger. "*Actually*, I said a decade *tops.*" He glanced at his wrist. There was no watch. "And, by my estimations, it's been ten days. I'm no mathematician, but ten days is marginally shorter than a decade."

He had Greg there. Greg pursued an alternate line of attack. "Our shop was on fire!"

Dewin looked at the fire engines and the brigade, clad in helmet and uniform.

"I told you not to panic. Haven't you ever cared for a phoenix before?"

Donum Ex Deo

"Well, what do you think?"

"Uh…"

"You do like it, don't you?"

"Well…"

"Wonderful! I'm so glad you're pleased. You know, I was wondering about whether it was the *right* gift or not, and — you know — you can never tell!"

"Right…" As the word tumbled from my mouth, the box in my hands shuddered a bit. Not much, gosh *no*, but enough that I noticed it. And… was that a little squeak? I couldn't be sure of that last one, because *they* kept talking.

"So, what do you say?" said one of the ones with wings. I got a distinct impression it wanted to please the big one.

"I— *what?*"

"What do you say?" It nodded encouragement.

"Um, *thank you?*"

Its immediate smile told me I had given the right answer. And then the big one clapped its hands, which made me jump. "Go ahead, try it on for size!" said the giver of the gift. I couldn't quite make the face of that one out, due to the blinding light. Its voice was deep and booming, yet it somehow *comforted* me — in its weird way.

"Right… right *now?*"

"No time like the present!" The cheer contained within that voice made my insides shrivel. It thought it had done well. It was *happy.* How could I shatter its illusion? How it *didn't* know I didn't *love* the present was beyond me. Wasn't that part of its schtick? I searched my mind, tried to remember the old mumblings. I for sure thought it was capable of knowing, and yet…

"Okay," I said. My voice was *very* small, and — even to my ears — sounded a long way away.

"Fantastic!" said the big one. There was a click of fingers. "You can find a changing room behind you — we'll give you some privacy! But be sure to come out and show us when you're ready." I could hear the smile on its face, even though I couldn't *quite* make out its face. That damn light.

I turned around and sunk into the fluffy floor. True enough, there was a changing room *right there*. Had it been there when I arrived? I had no idea, I couldn't remember. And speaking of arrivals and faulty memories — *how* had I gotten here in the first place? And *when?* And *why?* I twisted my neck around to ask one of them — *any* of them. But then I locked eyes with one of the winged fellows and thought better of it. Its expectant face told me they were all excited and they were all waiting.

For me.

I sighed and trudged into the changing room. I shut the door behind me and slid the lock across with a wooden *clack!* Despite the barrier between me and *them*, I still felt exposed. Vulnerable. *Naked.* I know that sounds silly because everyone says they're quite nice. And yet I felt those things, nonetheless.

I looked at the box in my hands. Yep, there was something in there. It rustled and yipped. Something *alive*. I knew what it was in the same way I know what plankton is — I know it's a thing. But I couldn't tell you about its shape or form or draw it for the life of me. Nightmarish visions crept into my already fragile mind. "Oh, God…" I whispered, then opened the damned thing.

I wasn't prepared for the thing that leapt out. It sprang from its prison right at me, squealing and jabbering. I caught the briefest of glimpses of it before it hit me in the face. It looked like a bloody scab, a flurry of television static, a spider, and an octopus all at the same time.

And then the world (if that's the word I should use) went dark as it struck me and knocked me off my feet. The floor was soft, and I suffered no injuries as I sank into the white fluff. I opened my mouth to scream as the *thing* on my face writhed and squirmed and struggled and thrashed and squeaked and chattered.

Big mistake.

The ball of mess forced its way into my mouth. My tongue and inner cheeks fuzzed and tingled with pins and needles. Before I could react, the little terror had disappeared down my throat. For one moment, I thought I wouldn't be able to breathe. But the gulp of air that followed soon exposed the falseness of this notion.

I lay there on the cotton wool floor of the changing room that hadn't been there when I arrived. The bugger made a home in the cavity of my chest. I could feel it, as it twisted and knotted and muttered away inside my chest. It coiled and turned around incessantly. I remained there for half a minute, rubbing my torso as if to burp. Occasional twangs as it pushed against my heart and lungs.

A rap of unhuman knuckles against the door startled me.

"Um, excuse me? Sir? Are you all right in there?"

I cleared my throat and suppressed the urge to vomit. "Yes. Quite all right. Coming out in a moment. Just two ticks."

"Oh, okay. I'll let the big guy know."

I swallowed. *Hard.* To try and quell the buzz in my upper body. I forced myself to sit upright and marvelled at how soft the floor felt. *It* still chittered away beneath my ribcage. The bones of my body amplified the vibrations. With a groan, I staggered to my feet. I was okay once I was upright, save for one nasty moment when a wave of acidity rose at the back of my throat.

I swayed for a second. The weight of the world (I'm still unsure if that's the right word) pressed in at me from all angles. My heart thrummed inside my chest, a bird in a cage. It fluttered against the bars. My lungs burned, and I couldn't *quite* get enough air. As if I'd run a marathon. I ran my fingers across my sweat-slaked palms. Damp perspiration clung to the back of my neck and moistened the shirt beneath my armpits. Hot and cold — an awful combination of the two. I *want* to say I had no idea what was happening to me, but that would be a lie.

I knew exactly what it was.

With a *click-clack*, I undid the lock on the changing room door and pushed it open. I gave myself no time to prepare. Somehow, I knew if I didn't *do it* and get it over and done with, I never would.

"Ah, there he is!" said the one who'd bestowed the box upon me. "We'd begun to wonder if you'd fallen asleep in there!"

I smiled in response. "Nope." It was all I could think to say.

"So…?" asked the one with a light-obscured face. "How does it feel?"

"Um…" I dragged out the syllable for as long as possible, I didn't want it to end. As long as I *umm*-ed, I wasn't telling it that I hated the gift. But, as with all good things, my *um* came to an end. "I feel… *different*, I guess," I said. Lame.

The big one clapped its hands again. "Different! Ha! Yes, that's the truth, isn't it?" It clapped its hands again. "Ha! Yes, yes… *different!* And *I* should know — I made it, after all, didn't I?

"You made it?"

"Well, of course I did, or my name isn't—"

"You made it to do the things it does?"

A slight pause. "Why would I make it not do the things it does?"

I frowned.

It continued. "I didn't make it to do things it doesn't, did I?"

I tilted my head to one side, in imitation of a puppy confused by a noise. "I guess?" I said, unsure how to proceed.

"Ha! Only pulling your leg!" said the giver of gifts. "Of course I made it do the things it does. If I hadn't, then who would've? And if I hadn't made it, I wouldn't be giving it to you, would I?"

"I suppose not."

One of the winged fellows started to say something. "Any…" It cleared its throat. "Mmh, any, um, *side-effects?*"

"Side-effects?"

"Oh, you know. Shortness of breath. Heart palpitations. Excessive sweating. Irritability. Inability to focus. An ever-present fear of the moment and how future events will unfold…" It trailed off. "You know — that sort of thing."

"Well, I—"

"Oh, don't be silly! I designed the gift in the manner that I designed it, and that's that." The big one grinned from ear to ear despite its obscured facial features. "There's no—" it raised its hands to do mock air quotations "—*side-effects*. All of the effects are entirely intended."

"Yes, yes, of course, I'm sorry, it's just that—"

The big one interrupted the smaller one again. "Now, now, I think we've taken up more than enough of this chap's time, don't you?"

"Yes, but before he goes I should check—"

"Excellent! Now, shall we stick our little present back in its box, so that you can take it home safely?" The smaller one with wings deflated and took a step backwards with a huff.

I looked down at my torso. "I don't know how to, I'm afraid. I think it's inside my chest."

"Here." The big one took a step closer. "Allow me." Before I could stop it, it shoved its hand down my throat. Unlike the thing that looked like television static and a spider, it wasn't unpleasant. It wasn't *pleasant*, by any stretch of the imagination, but it wasn't traumatic and discomforting. A second later, it pulled the squirming, jabbering thing out of me, shoved it back in the box and slammed the lid shut. "I'd keep this closed until you get back down there," it said with a smile. I couldn't *see* the smile, but boy could I *hear* it. It then tried to pass the box back to me.

"I don't— I mean, do I *have* to?"

I sensed the big one frown. "*Have* to?"

The smaller winged ones shuffled their feet (if that's the right word for whatever they had at the end of their legs). I had made things awkward.

"You don't like it?" it asked.

My chest began to feel tight, and I'm not ashamed to say I panicked. "No, I love it!" I all but shouted and gestured for it to give me the infernal gift. I didn't want the thing inside the box, and I *certainly* didn't want the thing inside the box inside *me*. But, more than all those things, I didn't want to upset this benevolent being. I didn't want to make it sad. I didn't — nay, *couldn't* — tell it I didn't like its gift. Even if it was a bloody terrible one.

"Grand!" It perked up again. "I thought for a second there… Oh, no, never mind. Here." It thrust the container at me once more. I took it. Almost immediately, the thing inside squirmed and fought within its cubic prison. It could sense my proximity. The thought churned my stomach.

I smiled. "Thank you. Very much!" I hoped my enthusiasm sounded more sincere than it felt. I wondered whether the big one could sense my falseness. If it did, it didn't say so.

"You're very welcome," it said. "Now, I expect you're itching to get back, aren't you?"

"Well," I weighed the box in my hands, "I guess." I cleared my throat. "Although, I'm not *entirely* sure on how to do that. Sorry." The tacked-on apology felt very clumsy as it tumbled out of my mouth.

"Not a problem," said the big one, whose face I *still* couldn't make out. I suppose I never *would* be able to make it out. I think that's kind of the whole point. "Take the escalator." It gestured with one of its massive hands.

I turned around and wasn't shocked to discover the changing room was now an escalator. The handrail was golden and shiny. "Oh, I didn't see it there," I said. The one who'd given me the present chuckled in response. "Well, in that case, I guess I better…" I nodded towards the exit. "Thanks for everything. It was a pleasure to meet all of you — really lovely."

"You're more than welcome. I look forward to seeing you

soon — although, not *too* soon, of course!" At that, the big one bellowed a volley of laughter. The smaller ones with wings offered some meek chuckles and chortles. They *might* have been pity laughs, but I couldn't be sure.

On the journey from the clouds — towards my body tucked under a duvet — I inspected the enclosure. The little box had three words stamped on it. The last two were 'FROM GOD', with a little cross to mark a kiss beneath. It was sweet when you thought about it. Well, if you thought about it but didn't think about it *too much*, that was. The preceding word described the contents of the box — the gift from the big guy upstairs:

'ANXIETY'.

Earth.exe

His name — although he'd later forget it — was Jerome Hodgson.

He woke up on an April morning to the bleat of his alarm. He silenced his digital friend, although it was more of a foe, and swung his legs out of bed. He slipped into his slippers and plodded his way downstairs.

Jerome popped the kettle on, pulled a mug out of the cupboard and opened the jar of the instant coffee he liked. He spooned a dollop of the brown flakes into the cup, along with a spoon of sugar. The cartoon cat on the side of the ceramic looked at him with bleary eyes. 'GO AWAY, I'M STILL ASLEEP.'

As the kettle whistled, Jerome bent down and pulled the carton of milk out of the fridge. The switch on the kettle clicked. Jerome poured the boiled liquid into the mug, where it intermingled with the contents. Jerome closed his eyes and inhaled the aroma. "Best smell in the world," he said to the empty house.

He then poured the milk.

Or at least, he tried.

He unscrewed the little green cap and set it on the counter. He lifted the plastic carton. The liquid began to dribble out, a paperwhite waterfall. The first drips splashed into the copper-black coffee.

And then stopped.

Jerome, who'd woken two minutes ago and had not had his required caffeine fix, blinked at the frozen cascade of milk.

His hand lingered in the same position, as did the carton.

But the milk didn't move.

It remained suspended in midair, a link between bottle and mug. Motionless.

Jerome frowned. He tilted the carton at a more acute angle.

And found that he couldn't.

The bottle was stuck in the air, a beetle pinned to an entomologist's corkboard.

Jerome tugged at it, but it refused to budge.

"What the—"

Jerome let go and took a step back. As if the whole scene might explode at any second.

The carton of milk waited in the air, with its milk in suspended animation. It looked like one of those pretentious art projects.

Jerome blinked at the scene. He reached forward and tapped the carton.

It didn't move.

And, even more curious, it no longer felt like damp plastic and cardboard with a liquid inside. It felt rigid, like marble.

His finger extended like E.T., Jerome moved his hand to the milk. He flicked it with his nail.

The liquid — if you could call it such — didn't react. His nail hit the surface in the same manner that it'd hit a stone. Only there was no audible confirmation, as there would have been with a harder substance.

"What the…?" Jerome looked around. But, of course, there was nobody to exchange a glance of confusion with. He lived alone. His eyes darted to the corners of the room. No cameras, nothing to show this was an elaborate prank.

With a hand that trembled, he grasped the handle of the mug and tried to lift it. It felt as if he'd super glued it to the countertop. Only he'd never do that because it was granite and had been expensive. He raised an eyebrow at the mug.

"What the hell?"

He braced himself, screwed his eyes shut, and dipped a finger into the boiling coffee.

Only he didn't.

The tip of his digit collided with the surface. It felt like glass and not hot at all.

Eyes wide, hair still messed up from sleep, Jerome rested his hands on his hips. At least those felt as fleshy — and doughy — as they'd always felt. He was about to complete his quartet of *What the hells* when a sound stopped him.

It was a noise he recognised, although Jerome couldn't pinpoint from what.

It was also rather difficult to say where the noise came from. It seemed to bleed out of the pores of the air itself, above and below and around him on all sides.

He glanced out of the kitchen window. In the garden, nothing twitched. No birds flew. No squirrels scrambled through hedges. The leaves of the trees didn't tremble in a Spring morning breeze. The blades of grass — which, he admitted, needed a cut — didn't sway with a tickle of the wind.

Oblivious to his current attire of pink pyjamas, Jerome ran for his front door. He slammed it open and stumbled out onto his front step. He'd made it halfway across his lawn when he stopped, mouth agape in an 'O' of surprise.

The other houses, the rest of the neighbourhood, were gone. The land stretched out before him, featureless.

No hills, no mountains, no trees, valleys, hedges, nothing. Utter smoothness, as perfect as the surface of a marble. An off-white marble — all the colours had gone, too.

Jerome's gaping jaw sunk to his chest with a click.

And again came that sound, this time in rapid succession. Again, it seemed to stream through the pinholes in the fabric of the universe.

Jerome was able to put his finger on it now. As someone who'd worked in IT all his life, he should have picked up on it sooner.

It was the *Nuh-huh, something's gone wrong, Boss* noise a PC makes. When a program has crashed or frozen and the broken software holds the rest of the computer hostage.

Again and again, the sound thunked out across the blankness. As if someone clicked a mouse button in vexation with the non-functioning machine.

Jerome's heart throbbed at the base of his throat. He tried to swallow and found he couldn't. For one stuttered microsecond, he thought he had stopped too. He'd choke to death, asphyxiate on his organ. But then the saliva went backwards and his breaths rushed in and out again.

He turned and fled for the safety of his house. Broken physics or not, it was a damn sight better than this planet made up of unmarked paper. This dull pearl of a globe, with no colour and no landscape. With its unnatural smoothness as far as the eye could see.

Jerome lost a slipper in the process, but he didn't care. All he wanted was to be inside and to shut the door. To lock it, in case this disease of nothingness could spread. Double lock it. To pull the chain ac—

Jerome ran smack into nothing and bounced off. He landed smack on his arse with a thud. Warmth trickled down his upper lip and his face throbbed. He brought a hand up to his nose and winced at the spark of pain. He winced again when he took his fingers away and saw blood.

"Owb. By nobe."

Jerome sat on his front step and prodded at his poor nose. He didn't think he'd broken it. For the moment, his surprise and pain distracted him from the blanket of dirty snow.

He frowned at the open doorway. He'd not shut the door when he left. What on Earth had he run into?

He staggered to his feet, drunk. He left a bloodied handprint on his front step. Like a man in the dark, Jerome fumbled around in front of him and took micro-steps forward.

At first, there was nothing. Nothing, as in, nothing he could have collided with. But as he reached the doorframe's threshold, his fingers touched something solid.

A wall.

"How in the…?"

Jerome pushed himself up against the clear boundary. He felt along, up and down it. His fingers searched, his palms swished. The world's greatest mime act.

There was no break or gap in the wall, nor was there any give.

Jerome banged his fists against the surface. His clenched hands made no noise as they slammed against the nothingness.

"Let me in!" He surprised himself by screaming. "Let me in! It's my house, so let—" he hit the wall "—me—" he slapped it "—in! Do what you want with the rest of it, just leave me at home. Leave me in peace!"

But the wall did not budge.

And the world around remained blank.

Again, the error tone pinged through the world. Again and again and again, a celestial finger rapped a tattoo against the mouse button.

Jerome sank to his knees, bloodied and defeated. He hadn't so much as left a crimson smear on the transparent force field.

How long he remained there, he had no idea. He sobbed and he sat. And his breaths rushed in and out like a waterfall. The world around him washed away. And then, he felt himself begin to fade as well.

He inhaled. The muscles in his extremities relaxed. He exhaled, all physical sensation dimmed. He breathed in, and his mind let all go. He breathed out, and all memory of who he was, what the world should be, and what his place was in it drifted away. A nebulous fog ushered along by a gentle kiss of wind.

After a time, a voice echoed through the air. The molecules necessary for the conduction of sound were still functional. Jerome lifted his head and perked up, ears attuned. "God?" he whispered to his doormat.

But God was in conversation with someone else.

"Yes, I've tried that, and it's still not working. Honestly, I don't know why I ever swapped, everything worked fine with my old one. The salesperson assured me that—"

An unintelligible voice murmured something.

"Yes, of course it's all turned on. I'm not a moron, you know!"

The fuzzed-out voice mumbled something else.

"What? Seriously, that's your best advice? 'Have you tried turning it off and on again?'" The omnipresent voice sighed.

"Yes, all right, I'll give it a shot, but if this doesn't work I'll demand a refund. You know—"

Darkness.

* * *

His name was Jerome Hodgson.

He woke up on an April morning to the bleat of his alarm. He silenced his digital friend, although it was more of a foe, and swung his legs out of bed. He slipped into his slippers and plodded his way downstairs.

Jerome popped the kettle on, pulled a mug out of the cupboard and opened the jar of the instant coffee he liked. He spooned a dollop of the brown flakes into the cup, along with a spoon of sugar. The cartoon cat on the side of the ceramic looked at him with bleary eyes. 'GO AWAY, I'M STILL ASLEEP.' read the speech bubble.

As the kettle whistled, Jerome bent down and pulled the carton of milk out of the fridge. The switch on the kettle clicked. Jerome poured the boiled liquid into the mug, where it intermingled with the contents. Jerome closed his eyes and inhaled the aroma. "Best smell in the world," he said to the empty house.

He then poured the milk. As he did so, a vague memory of something unpleasant touched the back of his mind. The chilled caress of a nightmare half-submerged in the inner waters. The fuzzy shape of a forgotten word on the tip of the tongue. And then the milk swirled with the blackness to form a rich copper colour, and Jerome forgot all about it.

Jerome lifted the mug and sighed. He took a sip of his beverage and stared out at the activity in the garden. Birds tweeted and flew. Squirrels scrambled beneath the hedges. The leaves of the trees danced in a spring breeze. The blades of grass swayed to nature's gentle waltz.

Life was good.

Feel Like Baking Love

The illuminations of Nocte Urbis flashed red, green, and gold.

A few of the lights were icicle-blue, a purplish sheen imbued with the frost. The crowd shuffled in the snow — hats on heads, scarves around necks, mittens on hands. The flakes fell with relaxed ease — they were in no rush, they had all the time in the world.

Mayor Frank gripped the podium, the bolts in his neck replaced with striped candy canes. "Ladies and gentlemen! Thank you all so much for coming out in such force this fine December evening. It's wonderful to see so many of you! Lots of old faces — Drac, I'm looking at you!" Frank bellowed a volley of laughter, as did the crowd. "And a few new ones, too." The eight-foot-tall man smiled at his audience. His forehead was cavemanlike. Stitches and staples were visible at the joins in his green flesh.

Thomas Walker watched from the far edge of the crowd, arms crossed. Two elongated teeth hooked over his lower lip. Despite his air of recent grumpiness, a smile tugged at the corners of his mouth. The lights from his shop cast a warm orange glow on the blanket of white that cushioned the ground. The sign above the door said 'BLOODY GOOD'.

"And we're here tonight," Frank gestured at the greenery behind, "to light this Christmas tree!" A round of applause, cheers and hoots. Delirious and cheerful. "Felled by the multitalented Mr Yeti." The mayor pointed into the crowd. "There he is, folks! He's shy, so be sure to give him a round of applause and tell him your thanks!" Mr Yeti blushed and waved a booklet of Christmas hymns — tiny in his humungous paw.

Anna Von smiled at the new faces, most of whom she'd yet to meet. Several of her treats were in circulation in the crowd, given out for free to try and drum up business. A stylised calligraphic font out front read 'Soul Food'. The ghost eyed the vampire across the way, arms folded, face stony. They'd had an altercation the day before, but they'd settled into a ceasefire. For the time being, at least.

"...and with thanks to our more nimble and winged friends for putting the lights up," said Mayor Frank. The faeries, goblins, gnomes and leprechauns danced over the branches of the pines. Small squeaks and cheers. One or two of the more fastidious creatures altered a bauble here and adjusted a light there. "Now, for our resident tinkerer, Dr Mad Scientist. Mad, if you'd do the honours of turning on the lights!"

Mad grinned and waved at the mayor. He'd altered his genes — to last a month, or so he predicted — to give himself antlers and a shiny red nose. To get into the holiday spirit. He raised his finger.

"TEN, NINE, EIGHT, SEVEN," said the crowd, led by Frank.

Dr Scientist lowered his finger.

"SIX, FIVE, FOUR, THREE."

Anticipation in the air.

"TWO, ONE..."

Mad hit the switch, and the Christmas tree *thumped* into life. Bulbs dazzled, colours flared. Glitter twinkled, gold and silver. The lights winked in and out of existence. The crowd *oohed* and *ahhed* and rained thunderous applause upon Dr Scientist. Overhead, the dragons breathed flames — red, orange, green, blue — into the winter's night.

Frank extended his arms — a wingspan of almost ten feet. "Let the festivities begin!"

"And a-one, and a-two, and a-one-two, three, four..." The zombies groaned into the night. Their choir was a backdrop for the banshees, who wailed their carols in harmony.

After a slight pause, the crowd joined in. Werewolves with baubles hooked into their fur began to howl, the melody one we all know. Mummies — bandages exchanged for wrapping paper — moaned along. Not quite as rehearsed as the choir, but with more than enough enthusiasm. Unicorns, Christmas lights wrapped around their horns, stomped their hooves and whinnied. Basilisks with tinsel twisted around their bodies slithered over the ground. They hissed their good cheer. Giants and orcs and ogres and cyclopses with Santa hats began to mill about. They laughed amongst friends, mugs of hot chocolate and gluhwein in hand.

Thomas sighed. He shut his shop door and flipped the sign around. 'SORRY, WE'RE OPEN' became 'COME ON IN, WE'RE CLOSED'. The bell overhead tinkled on his way out. The vampire raised his cloak to his eyes and stole through the crowd.

"Hey, how we doing tonight?"

"Yeah, Merry Christmas to you too!"

"Haha, yeah, it sure is!"

"Glad you're liking 'em, I'll bake more tonight!"

"Ooh, I love that outfit. Make it yourself?"

"Yeah, happy holidays!"

"I know, brr, right? Hear it's gonna get down to the minuses tomorrow!"

He broke free of the throng on the other side and came face to face with the ghost. The pair eyed each other for a moment, the vampire and the spirit. Anna hovered six inches above the ground, shop visible through her translucent body.

"Hello, Anna," he said.

"Thomas." The ghost nodded.

The vampire looked up at the snow that fell. "Lovely weather we're having, hm? Looks to be a white Christmas."

Anna followed his gaze. "Hmm. Quite."

An awkward silence fell over them.

"You here to chew me out again?"

He smiled. "No, Anna. I came to say that I'm sorry."

Anna looked shocked for a moment. "Oh."

"I've thought about what I said, and it doesn't make any sense."

"That you'd get annoyed over a bakery that doesn't even cater to the same kind of customers as your own?"

Thomas watched as a ghost floated past, a ghost cookie in hand. He nodded. "Yeah, something like that." He sighed. "So, yeah, I'm sorry. Truce?"

Anna nodded. "Truce."

Another moment of silence.

Anna cleared her throat. "So, what was it? Holiday grumpiness? Pre-January blues?"

Thomas let his gaze drop to the snow on the ground between them. A billion flakes of glitter twinkled their reflections of the Christmas lights. "No, I don't think it was that at all." The vampire swallowed the spit that had accumulated in his mouth. "You know how kids on the playground can be mean to those whom they like?" He raised his eyebrows but continued to stare at their feet. Or, rather, *his* feet and *her* ghost mist that petered away into nothing.

"Yeah?"

She hadn't understood.

Thomas raised his face — it was a great effort. As if stuck in treacle. "Well…"

"Oh." Anna's eyes widened. "Oh!"

Thomas blushed. The colour in his cheeks was rather strange. "Sorry."

A fluttered heartbeat.

Her voice softened. "Don't be."

His dead heart trembled and stumbled over its step. Was it too absurd to read reciprocation in that warmth? Was it so crazy to hope? To dream? Shoot for the moon. If you miss, you'll land in the cold void of space with no oxygen to breathe. Which will be fine, because you're a vampire and you're undead.

Thomas hooked a thumb in the direction of his store. Baked treats infused with human blood were ready to take out of the oven. "I've gotta get back. Busy season, and all."

Anna smiled at him — a proper one. There was nothing perfunctory or businesslike about it.

"Listen, Anna…"

"Yes, Thomas?"

"Would it be — and please, be honest here, I won't be offended. In fact, I think I know what the answer will be, which will be okay. I mean, you're allowed to make your own decisions, and I don't want to be presumptuous. It's just that, well, if you never take your shot, you'll never score, will you?"

The vampire rushed to correct himself. "Not that I think of being with you will be scoring — gosh no, I just—"

"I'd love to. How about coffee, once we're both closed up for the evening? We can talk. Properly, this time." She offered him a grin. "No more hair-pulling."

"I—"

"Get back to your shop, Thomas." Anna winked at him. "We'll talk later."

Thomas nodded, tongue wrapped into knots at the back of his mouth. He smiled at her. "Merry Christmas, Anna."

The ghost smiled back.

"Merry Christmas, Thomas."

George, Jenny, and the Stars

"Charlotte, I'd like to go into the attic, please."

"No problem, George," came the pleasant response. All her responses were pleasant.

There were a few beeps, followed by a series of mechanical clicks. George stepped back as the ladder unfolded down. "Thanks, Charlie."

"You are most welcome, George."

He climbed the steps and took care as he ascended. His joints creaked with age. By the time he reached the top, he was out of breath. "Oh dear, George, old boy…"

"Is something the matter, George?"

"No, nothing Charlie. Just old age." He nodded to himself. "Just old age…" George smiled as if half-remembering something lovely. He stepped into the attic. "Charlie?" he asked.

Lights bloomed overhead. "It is quite dusty up here, George. Would you like me to call a cleaner?"

George waved the comment away. "Naw, I'll get around to it at some point, Charlotte. Leave it to me."

"As you wish, George."

He scanned the room. "Now, where did I…?"

"Can I help you, George?"

"Nah, just let me think, Charlie"

77

"Sorry, George. I'll let you get on with it."

"My memory's not what it used to be. Takes me time to get the old thinker going."

"I understand George."

There were boxes stacked as high as the ceiling dotted all around the attic. A few scattered on the floor, half-opened. Their contents spilled out — as if someone had abandoned a search midway through. There were several old tables and chests of drawers and one old wardrobe. A handful of old chairs accompanied these pieces of furniture. At the far end of the room was a large circular window, through which yellow light poured. Dust floated through the sunbeams like fairy powder.

George wandered the attic, looking from each stack of boxes to the next. Now and then, he peered into one of the opened boxes on the floor. Charlotte sighed.

"Maybe over here…"

George pulled a chair across to one of the stacks of boxes that tickled the underside of the ceiling. The heavy thing groaned against the wooden floor as the old man dragged it. Once it was in position, George nodded to himself. He began to pull himself up onto the chair.

"George, please be careful," said Charlotte.

"I'm fine." George gasped as pulled himself upright.

"Please, George."

"Quit nagging me, damn it!"

"I'm sorry George. I just worry."

George's shoulders sagged. "Yeah, I know. Sorry, Charlie. Didn't mean to snap."

"It's okay, George. But please do watch what you're doing. I don't want you to hurt yourself."

78

"I'll be careful, I'll be careful…"

He reached for the highest box. His arthritic fingers grasped the underside of the carboard, and George pulled. He almost had it, and then his strength sagged, as it was wont to do. The box slipped out of his grip and dropped to the floor. Its contents scattered in every direction.

"Ah, piss it!"

"George, language!"

"Sorry, Charlie. Not appropriate in front of a lady, I know."

George got down from the chair. There was a heart-stopping moment where he almost fell over, but then he regained his balance. He hobbled over to the upended crate, and shook his head with a mutter. He winced as he bent down and began to place things back into the box. He examined each item as he did so.

Charlotte watched as George knelt there and mumbled to himself. Or maybe he was talking to her. Sometimes, it was hard to tell. Truth be told, she worried what this would do to his knees. She hoped he'd be able to get back up again. Charlotte watched until George paused for a minute.

"Now this… this I definitely remember." It wasn't clear if he spoke to Charlotte or himself. He lifted something small into the air. Charlotte zoomed in. It looked to be the stub of a ticket. "I was 17." He looked up and grinned. The smile made him look ten years younger. "Seventeen! Now that's a good age. Good age, isn't it? Seventeen?"

"Seventeen is a good age, George," agreed Charlotte. "What's it from?"

George looked down at the stub, which he cradled as if it would crumble and fade if he were too rough with it.

"George?"

"Best day of my life," said the old man, voice barely above a whisper. He looked up at Charlotte. "It was our first date, you know?"

"With Jenny?"

George laughed. "Of course, with Jenny. She was the only girl I ever dated." He snapped his fingers. "I met her, and then BAM! I knew she'd be the only girl I'd want to be with for the rest of my life."

George squinted at the date, stamped at the top right-hand-side. He whistled through his teeth. "Sixty-seven years ago. Sixty-seven!" He shook his head. "Doesn't seem right," he muttered.

"What was the ticket for, George?"

"The Shooting Star," said George, with reverence. "Scariest goddamn rollercoaster ever built. No matter what anyone says, nothin' these days can even touch it. The Shooting Star…"

* * *

George sat down with a sigh.

Charlotte noticed him wince as he seated himself, but George seemed unaware. The ticket stub entranced him. "It was the first ride of its kind to exit the atmosphere. Did you know?"

"I did, George. It was a remarkable feat of human engineering."

"It was. It was." George nodded. He seemed to get lost in his thoughts for a while. "I had asked her out during school. I was so scared!" He cackled. "My palms wouldn't stop sweating, and I couldn't control the pitch of my voice. It was up and down, up and down, up and down." George waved his hand around, to emphasise his point.

"But she said yes?" asked Charlotte, eager to get George to keep talking. It was good for him.

"Ha! Yes, she did! Yes, she did!" George smiled. "But I was so certain that she would turn me down. She was gorgeous! And so cool, sophisticated… I was just this awkward guy who shared some of her classes. Why would she care about me? I didn't think she'd even know who I was! But when I asked her, not knowing where to look, she smiled. Man, she had such a nice smile. Her eyes just lit up, you know?"

"I know, George."

"They were the darkest brown. Like chocolates. And she'd get these little dimples in her cheeks…" George trailed off. "Where was I, again?"

"You were saying that Jenny said yes to your proposal for a date."

"Ah, yes!" George slapped his knee and laughed. "She said yes! She even blushed! Her! Jenny! Blushing over me! I tell you, I felt on top of the world as I walked away. I felt like I could conquer the world then, I tell you!"

George paused and looked off into the distance. Charlotte pushed him on. "And then what happened, George?"

"Well, that was a Tuesday, and our date was for the Friday. I skipped classes for the rest of the week, as I was petrified we'd bump into each other and she'd cancel the date! So then Friday came… and it was magical. Just… magical." George grinned and leant back into the chair. "We met at the park. I was too afraid to meet her parents, you understand?"

"I understand, George. It can be quite a nerve-wracking experience."

"It certainly can be! Well, we met at the park, and the stars were already out. The lights from the rides cast a beautiful

81

glow over everything, and she was just the prettiest thing I had ever seen."

"And you went straight to the rollercoaster? The Shooting Star?"

"Gosh, no! Truth be told, I was petrified of that damn thing! Had never ridden it before that night. I just wanted to look brave in front of my Jenny." George paused. "Well, she wasn't my Jenny then. Not yet, anyway."

"So, what did you do?"

"We walked around, talking. About nothing in particular. Books. Movies. School. Exams. The future. I tried to make it seem like I had everything figured out, university, careers… I didn't know a damn thing! I just wanted to look impressive… adult. We did all the little games, you know? The ones where you fire lasers at the space aliens, and if you hit enough o' them you get some sweets. Probably seems a bit racist now, but that's how it was then."

"A tad racist, George. But they were different times. Before humans mastered intergalactic travel."

"True, true." George watched the dust float through the golden shaft of light. It had shifted since he began the arduous climb to the attic. "I won her some candyfloss. I think she could have probably won some herself — she was definitely a better shot than me, as I later found out — but I guess she didn't want to embarrass me. She always thought about those kinds of things. Sweet woman."

"And then you went on the ride?"

"Haha, yes! Although I was completely terrified!"

"But you wanted to look brave, correct?"

George looked up, surprised. "Exactly! She was scared to go on The Shooting Star, so I had to make it seem as if I wasn't scared of anything. Well, I managed to convince her that it'd be a good idea. And she said, 'George, are you sure it's safe?' and I said, 'Absolutely!' So, we bought a couple of tickets—" the old man lifted the ticket stub "—and got in line."

George looked at Charlotte. "Well, there we were, waiting in line. She was pestering and fussing. Absolutely scared witless. I felt a little bad, then. I didn't want to force her on to the ride if she really didn't want to do it. So, I said to her, 'Look, Jenny. If you don't want to go on the Shooter, we don't have to. But it'll be fine because I'm right here and I won't let anything happen to you.'"

"And what did Jenny say to that?" asked Charlie.

"Well, she didn't say a thing! She just looked up at me with those big, chocolatey eyes. And then she held my hand. Grabbed it, actually. And she held so tight. I tell you, I thought I was going to have a heart attack!"

"Did you actually suffer from a myocardial infarction at the age of 17?"

"Pardon?"

"Oh, no… That was a turn of phrase, wasn't it?"

"Come again, dear?"

"Never mind, George. So, back to your story. Jenny was holding your hand, and you were waiting in line for The Shooting Star."

"Right! Right. So, Jenny grabs my hand and looks up at me, and I knew she was going to give it a go. Never backed down from anything, that woman. So, it comes to our turn, and the guy at the ticket stand — couldn't have been more than a year older than us — says, 'Now's your chance to turn away, if you wanna.' Well, I looked down at Jenny, and she shook her head furiously. So, he leads us over to the seats, buckles us in, and tells us to enjoy the ride. Then he steps back and presses the button, and the bubble dome seals around us, and the ride starts moving. Y'know, clickety-clack, clickety-clack?"

"I know, George."

"And all this time, Jenny, bless her, hasn't let go of my hand. She's still gripping it, hard. And of course, I don't mind. I'm probably just as scared as she is! And I'm thinking to myself, 'This is the nicest thing I have ever held.' So, clickety-clack, the ride starts moving upwards. Once we're in position, it stops. And this big, boomin' voice comes on over the intercom." George began to imitate the voice. "'THREE. TWO. ONE. WE HAVE LIFTOFF!' And pow! We went rocketing up into the sky! Through the sky! Beyond the sky! I swore my stomach remained there back on earth at the rate we shot off! I could feel my heart in my throat! And Jenny—" George chuckled "—Jenny is clutching my hand so hard, her knuckles were white! I glanced over at her, worried, but she was smiling. Her eyes were wide, and she was smiling. And then we burst through, and we were among the stars."

George took a deep breath. Charlie noted that the smile hadn't left his lips the entire time he had recited the story. She let him take a break, and revel in the memory. "You know, back with the old tech, you could only stay out there without a suit for 20 seconds or so."

"Of course, the technology for prolonged exposure would come shortly after."

"Right, right. But those few seconds..." He gasped and shook his head. "It felt like an eternity. Just Jenny and me, suspended in the stars. Her hand in mine. And it was silent. Just, silence. For those few seconds." He grinned and looked at Charlie. "And that was when I knew."

"That was when you knew what, George?" she asked, curious.

"That she was the girl for me, of course!" George said, matter-of-factly.

"Oh, of course. Of course, George."

* * *

"It takes me back, y'know, Charlotte?"

He had sat there for some time. Charlotte worried about him getting back down the attic steps whilst tired. He got tired quicker and quicker these days.

"I know, George. I know." Charlotte considered the question for a split-second and then asked. "Will you keep searching, George? Perhaps you'll remember what it is you're looking for, this time."

George's eyes glazed over. "Looking for— what was I looking for? Was I looking for something?" The old man glanced at his surroundings. He seemed lost.

Charlotte sighed. "Nothing George. Never mind. Just me being silly."

George nodded, but he didn't seem sure of anything.

"Why don't we go back downstairs? I'll pop the kettle on, and we can have a nice cup of tea."

George smiled. "Now there's a plan, Charlotte. There's a plan!"

The old man descended the stairs with care. His joints creaked. Once he'd reached the ground floor, Charlotte raised the stairs. It always made her nervous, whenever he climbed up there. At the same time, in the kitchen, she filled the kettle with water and began to boil it.

With love, the A.I. that lived in the walls watched as George

85

pottered around the kitchen. He got two mugs and placed a teabag in each, as he always did. He had done so for 64 years, and it was a hard habit to break.

George muttered to himself. He smiled and shook his head as he pulled the sugar from the overhead cupboard. "Seventeen…"

Honesty in G# Minor

"Think of it like painting a picture."

"I can't paint, either."

"No, it doesn't matter. Just *think* of it like painting a picture."

"All right. But I still don't know how to paint a picture."

She sighed. "You don't need to be an art expert to know how to paint a picture. You have the foreground and the background, right?"

"Okay…"

"And the foreground is the most important bit, right?"

"Makes sense."

"The bit that everyone properly looks at?"

"Sure."

"But the background is *also* important — a bad background can ruin a good picture, but a great background can improve a picture. Right?"

"That also sounds about right. But I still don't see how that helps."

She grumbled but got a hold of herself. "It's *how* you think about the process, John."

"Okay, so, I'm painting a picture."

"Exactly."

"Without paints or a canvas or an easel."

"Precisely." A silence. "You don't get it, do you, John?"

"Not even slightly, Charlie."

"Gah! Okay, think of your favourite song."

"Oh, God... My *favourite* song? That's such a hard question..."

"Look, it doesn't have to be your *favourite*, just a song you *like*. A song you *know*."

"All right. *Stairway to Heaven*."

"No, that's a terrible example."

"*Stairway to Heaven* is a terrible song? Maybe you aren't the right teacher for me after all..."

"No, I didn't say it was a terrible *song*, I said it was a terrible *example*. Big difference, John. It's too complicated. Pick something simpler."

"Okay." He thought for a moment, face a rictus of thought. "*Sound of Silence?*"

"Ah, much better! Okay, think of the intro guitar." Charlie fingerpicked the first eight notes to the song. The melancholy voicings rang from the steel-string acoustic. The name on the headstock said 'Taylor'.

"Such a classic." John smiled as the familiar notes fell upon his ears.

"Right. Now, we all know the vocal melody and lyrics, right?"

"I should hope so." Together, the pair sang the opening line about darkness being a friend. Charlie continued to fingerpick the simple notes, her rhythm steady. They didn't harmonise — a fault which John took the blame for — but they didn't sound *horrendous*, either.

"Okay, so...?"

"So... *what?*"

"Do you see what I mean with background and foreground?" She picked the notes again. "Background." She sang the intro line about talking with an old friend again. Her voice followed the familiar melody with great ease.

Damn, John thought, *she sounds good.* He was jealous of her talent. Well, wasn't that why he had sought her out in the first place? They said she was good.

"Okay, I think I get it." John nodded. "Background and foreground."

Charlie beamed at him. Her smile lit up the room. "Great! Okay, so you get the idea of the *concept* of the bit at the front and the bit in the back."

"Yeah… sorta. But keep going."

She nodded. "Each is equally as important. A bad background can worsen a good foreground, and a bad foreground might mean that nobody even *looks* at your background." John gave her a quizzical look. "Okay, listen, Simon and Garfunkel again." Charlie picked the notes again, but this time, when she sang, she didn't follow the melody. She stuck to the same note, over and over again. She struck the same, monotonous pitch as the poetic lyrics danced onwards.

"That sounds *horrible!*" said John.

"*Exactly!* Your main melody — your *foreground* — is important. It needs to be simple enough for people to *get* it, yet original enough that people like it and enjoy it. It needs to stick in their minds."

"Okay. Crap melody, crap song. Gotcha. Use more than one note."

"Yeah. Sorta. Unless in special circumstances…" Charlie shook her head. Her hair whipped back and forth. "But don't worry about that, it'll just confuse you."

John stared at her for a moment, as if she were a crazy person. He nodded. "Let's not get ahead of ourselves. Just keep it simple for me, for the time being."

"Yeah. Baby steps, John, baby steps."

"Got it. So, carrying on, that bit's the foreground. What about the background bit you were harping on about?"

Charlie fingerpicked the intro chord to *Sound of Silence* again. "Okay, background — that's a D minor suspended chord. A D minor sus two, to be exact. Don't worry what that *means* for the time being. Now, listen to *this*." Charlie started to fingerpick again, only this time the notes didn't sound *quite* right.

John shook his head. "Nah, Charlie, you played it wrong that time."

She rolled her eyes. "I know. That was intentional, John. I'm playing a straight D minor chord. Notice how it doesn't have the same impact as…" She played the intro to *Sound of Silence* again.

"Right, right… The proper way sounds *cooler*." *God*, he thought, *am I getting too old to use the word 'cooler'?*

"—but I'm not saying you have to have a suspended chord as your intro chord, I'm just saying that an interesting background helps to make an interesting foreground. Harmony and melody together. They're the bread and butter of music. Get it?"

"Sure, when you put it like that. Why didn't you put it like that in the first place? Confusing me with paintings and all that…"

"Do you want my help or not?"

"Of course! I have to write a song for my wife."

"Because she says that you don't put in as much effort as you used to?"

"She hasn't said it that explicitly, but—"

"But you can tell that she *thinks* it."

"Well…" He trailed off. "How'd you know?"

"You're not the first husband who turned to the guitar to rekindle that marital spark, John."

"Oh."

"*Oh* indeed. So, do you want my help or not?"

"Yes, I do."

"That's good. Then listen to the advice I give and follow what I say."

"Couldn't you just write a song *for* me?"

"I *could*, but I *won't*."

"Damn. Why not?"

"Because it has to come from you. Music is all about honesty. A listener can tell whether you're being honest or not."

"They can?"

"Sure. Think of the classics. *Bohemian Rhapsody, Tiny Dancer, Comfortably Numb…* Every great song is written from a place of honesty. *Truthfulness.* Now, I'm not saying that Freddie Mercury actually *killed* a man, I'm just saying that when he sings those lines, you can tell he's singing from a place of pure intent. Got it?"

"Okay…"

"Now think of the worst song ever. I dunno, some generic love song from some ten-a-penny boy band. Y'know the type. They all sleep around with as many women as possible and then squeeze out painful lines about true love. Those lyrics stink like a bad fart, don't they?"

That made John roar with laughter. "They sure do!"

"Even if the music isn't all that bad. And why is that?"

"…because they're being dishonest?"

"*Yes!* You don't have to write complex or complicated stuff.

91

Just be honest. Say it from the heart. Play it from the soul. All of those clichés. If you're gonna sing it, you better bloody well *mean it.* They're called clichés because they're overused, not because they're untrue."

"Huh." John cocked his head to the side like a puppy. "Never thought of it like that."

"How long until your anniversary?"

"A month."

"Okay, that's doable. You'll be no Paul Simon or Art Garfunkel, but we can get you to a place where you're at the very least *semi*-decent. But you gotta work hard at it. So, pay attention."

"I *am!"*

"Sure. So, let's revisit the word you just used. You don't *have* to write a song for your wife. Going into a song with that mentality will make it cold, sterile. *Loveless.* You should *want* to write a song for your wife. It's a choice. A proclamation of love!"

John rolled his eyes. "All right, all right…"

"I know it's cheesy, but it's true. Sometimes, you gotta channel your inner cheese."

"My *inner cheese?"*

"Yeah, I know, it sounded better in my head. But you know what I mean, don't you?"

"I think so."

"Cool. So, I always find it's best to write lyrics when you already have the music and melody. I like to hum along and find that the right words sorta just… *slot* themselves in. But, we gotta find the right key for you."

"The right *key* for me?"

"Sure. No offence, John, but it takes a well-practised singer to sing in multiple keys. And even then, the pros tend to stick to the keys they know their voice works best with, after years of practice. Repeat after me: *La la la la la la la la!*" Charlie sang the eight rising notes with ease. She added some tasteful vibrato at the end of the octave.

John cleared his throat and repeated the phrase. His voice increased in pitch with each syllable. From the way Charlie winced, he could tell he didn't *quite* hit the right pitches.

"Hmm, nope, not E minor. Let's try..."

Several painful minutes later, they found it. "Yes, that's the one!"

"It is?"

"Yes!"

"I thought it sounded terrible."

"Well, you're no George Michael, but you hit those notes without straining too much. I think that'll do nicely."

"Huh. What key was that?"

"G-sharp minor."

"Sounds complicated."

Charlie shrugged and pulled a face. "It's not... not *really.*"

"Any songs I would know in... G whatsit?"

"G-sharp minor. I dunno, actually... I think *Don't Cry* by Guns N' Roses is in G-sharp minor... But don't quote me on that."

"Man, I *love* that song!"

"Well, now you know that you can probably sing it."

John nodded. He looked fairly impressed with himself. "So, what now?"

"Now we gotta get our chord pattern."

"Right... and how do I do that?"

"By knowing the emotion that you're trying to evoke."

"I dunno…" John wrinkled his nose. "I'm not sure what *emotion* I want to evoke."

"That's okay, let's just go by feel, okay?"

John nodded but seemed sceptical.

"Let's start with our root: G-sharp minor." Charlie strummed the chord. "Now, you try."

John squinted at her fingers. It took him a full three minutes to get his hand into the same shape as Charlie's. His fingers looked like a claw. When he strummed, the chord didn't sound *quite* as nice as Charlie's had, but he didn't think he had done too bad.

"Great! Now, there are *so* many directions we could go from here. First, let's look at an interval of a third…"

This is gonna take ages, thought John. But he felt good about himself. He felt hopeful that he'd walk away from this with something half decent. Something half *honest. After all, if it's worth doing…*

He smiled at the fresh calluses on the tips of his fingers.

* * *

He strummed the chord and then stopped.

"I feel silly."

"That's good."

"It is?"

"Yeah. If you feel awkward or embarrassed, that's because you feel *vulnerable. Open.* And that's how you should feel — be honest with your listeners, remember?"

"Yeah, but…"

"Look, it doesn't have to be poetry, okay? In fact, in my humble opinion, songs sound better when you *aren't* trying to be all poetic. It comes out crappy, and you end up stealing other people's clichés. Say what you want to say. Start with the basic building blocks. Once you've got that down, *then* we can try to make it flowery and pretty. If we *need* to, that is."

"Okay..."

"Just hum your melody, first of all. You still remember it?"

He did. He thought it was good. They'd written something that was neither derivative nor complicated. John thought it was pretty catchy. "Sure, I do."

"Play along, humming your melody. Think of the rhythms. The patterns. Syllables. Words that'd fit. Words that are important to you and your wife. Words that encapsulate your relationship. Places. Sounds. Smells. Feelings. Memories. Don't worry about rhyming for the time being. We'll burn that bridge when we get to it."

By now, John's fingers moved almost by muscle memory. He slid into the chord changes with *relative* ease. He couldn't play through the piece as smoothly as Charlie, but he could now play it all by heart. Most of the chords were simple, with some harder ones thrown in, to give the piece — in Charlie's own words — some *spice*. Chords with names that had 'suspension' or 'diminished' or 'minor seven' or 'add nine' or 'over C-sharp' in the title. John didn't know what they meant, but he knew how they *sounded,* and how they *felt.* Gentle and caressing. Soothing but not sad. Somehow sparkling and chiming — crystalline. In a word, *romantic*. He and Charlie strummed the intro chords. They were, for the most part, in time with each other. The two guitars chorused together.

John, a mechanic by trade, began to hum his melody. Never had he considered himself to be an 'artsy' person. But he was beginning to learn he could find satisfaction in this whole *creative pursuit* idea. He wished he'd picked up an instrument sooner, as opposed to half a century into his existence. *Better late than never, John old boy*, he told himself.

The guitars bounced from chord to chord. John's rough but endearing voice traced the melody. Like sections of a jigsaw that slot together, the words clicked into place. The lyrics and phrases fell upon him with an ease that shocked him — as if they descended from the heavens like rain. As the vague outline of the song began to take shape, he marvelled at the piece. It felt as though he were trapping a fragment of his very heart inside a bubble.

For the first time in *many* years, the prospect of giving his wife a gift excited him.

* * *

His voice wasn't perfect, and on many occasions, it cracked, wavered, or didn't strike the right pitch.

It didn't help that his mouth was dry — he felt nervous, like a young boy. In truth, he felt the same way that he had on their very first date, over 20 years ago. John thought that this was sensation was rather poetic; life had come full circle.

His guitar technique wasn't flawless. Sometimes he didn't press down on the barre chord and a string would buzz like an angry insect. Other times he'd slide up to a note and miss it — the clash of sounds cut through the body of the song like razor wire. John winced when these errors occurred, but he played on.

His rhythm wasn't completely steady, either. The song began at a solid 120 beats per minute and ended up at around 140. He wasn't sure how or when he'd sped up, but that final chorus was too fast. He chalked it up to nerves.

But on those glimpses between chord changes, when he stole a glance upwards, his heart did a backflip. She clasped her hands together and her watery eyes sparkled in the light. Her parted lips trembled — *oh so kissable*. The song *enraptured* her. Even when he slipped or tripped up, he kept going. He wanted that look to remain printed on her face forever. Even when the song tottered on the verge of implosion, he kept on strumming his cheap guitar. The one with the nylon strings.

And he sang to his wife.

A song of honesty.

In the key of G-sharp minor.

How to Build a Boat

I knew I was in for a spot of bother when the plane's wing exploded.

The aircraft gave a violent shudder as something *churned* (*krr-rrr, krr-rrr, krrrrr*). A few seconds of respite. And *KA-BOOM!*

I looked out of the passenger window as the thing blew up. First, a few licks of orange flames spat out of the engine. And then a detonation of dark reds and yellows and other autumnal hues. Dark, thick smoke plumed out of the turbine.

Everything after that was disordered chaos. Well, I suppose *all* chaos is disordered, but this was different forms of chaos intertwined. Screams — children, women, and men all shrieked at the top of their lungs. The alarms blared overhead. The air masks fell into our faces. I mean, I know they are there to help, but at the time it felt like a distraction. An insect in your face when you are trying to read the newspaper. And, of course, that awful *spinning* and *falling* sensation. It was unpleasant.

After that, I suppose my memory becomes a bit hazy. I remember the crunch of metal and the shatter of glass. I remember the screams *intensifying*. And I also seem to recollect some sort of explosion. It all feels a bit like a dream. I remember the terror, but it's quite hard to pinpoint the precise events and occurrences.

The next thing I knew, I woke up on a beach, my clothes soaked with seawater, my eyes red from the brine. Gulls chattered overhead, and the waves hushed a peaceful lullaby. The afternoon sun warmed my skin.

I winced in the bright light, unsure about *where the hell I was*. It all cleared in my mind, in fits and spurts. When the memory of the crash came back, vertigo seized me as if I were in freefall all over again.

I sat up and looked around. My head swizzled about, like a meercat. A sand-white beach stretched on for about a mile long. The roar of the sea on one side and dense rainforest on the other. A small river trickled through the trees, over the beach, and into the ocean. Its minuscule size in comparison to the vast body of water endeared it to me. I'd go as far as to say it was *cute*, a word I detest. To call it a river would be an *overstatement*; it was closer to a stream.

I staggered to my feet, a drunk who's slept off the booze in a gutter. I still wore my suit, but one of my leather loafers was gone. I damned the explosion. Those shoes had been expensive. Additionally, there were a few tears, here and there, on my attire. And a couple of scorch marks. I shook my head — what would my clients think of me now, were they to see me? No money would exchange hands that day, that's for sure.

I wobbled over to the stream, one shoe on, one shoe off, and crouched down. I was thirstier than I'd ever been, and whilst I was no outdoorsman, I knew I couldn't drink the water from the sea. I splashed my hands around in that rivulet and cleaned them of sand. The water was cool. I cupped a handful of the crystal-clear liquid and took a tentative sip from my palms, ready to spit it back out again. It was pleasant and refreshing

— no hint of salt.

In a fit of madness, I ducked my head into the water and gulped mouthfuls of the stuff as it swept my way. I only stopped when I opened my eyes to see a small fish darting out of the way to escape my gaped maw. Satiated, I leant back on the bank of the stream and gasped for breath. My hair dripped. My full belly sloshed.

As I sat there, I let my gaze wander upstream, into the trees. They were not as packed as I had thought. The sheer number of plants available had skewed my perception. The *vastness* gave the impression there was no room to breathe in the greenery, but that wasn't true at all. From my spot on the beach, I could see at least four different types of fruit as they hung from the trees. A good number of the bushes also sprouted berries and the like. Deep in the hidden depths of the forest, a bird that *wasn't* a seagull called out — exotic and beautiful.

The most wonderful sensation swept over me. I felt it all at once. As if someone had taken a brush and painted me in glitter in one great, sweep of a stroke.

The island was a veritable paradise.

Well, I say *island* because I have since discovered it to be so, but at the time I did not know where I was. But yes, it is (and was, of course) an island.

I'd like to say somebody Up There looked out for me, but if that were the case, I wouldn't have been there in the first place. Or I'd have woken up somewhere near civilisation, a location less than a 20-minute walk from my home. I also suppose you should take into account the other souls aboard that doomed plane. I often wonder what became of them.

No, the gorgeous sensation that took a hold of me — it was an unfathomable appreciation for the beauty of nature. It was as if I saw the Earth for the first time in my life. It took a plane crash to awaken in me a sense of thankfulness for this planet.

What I fool I had been.

* * *

As a man born of a certain time and age, I began to impose order upon my surroundings.

I built a shelter to protect myself from any tropical storms that might frequent the locale. Like a neighbour who pops over *uninvited.* For whom you must then make a cup of tea, for the sake of propriety.

The biggest issue was I had no prior experience in such activities. There was a vast amount of trial and error, something which I would have scoffed at.

In a previous life, my career had been my focus. What I *did* doesn't matter anymore. Know this, my friend. Every day I wore a suit, carried a briefcase, and crunched numbers. I clocked in at the office well before 9 a.m. and clocked out well after 5 p.m. It was a *different* existence.

And so, it took me several attempts to make, well, *anything.* I amassed a collection of leaves and twigs and branches and such. I had an idea of what my shelter could look like. Something ingenious, like from those fifties castaway movies. The main problem was the tremendous gulf between what I had in my mind and what I could *achieve.*

I figured out to lean the longest log I could find against one of the trees as a starting point. It took a lot of sweating and cursing and I earned an extra tear on the shoulder of my blazer. But I managed to get the thing up. I kicked it a few times, to make sure it wouldn't collapse on me whilst I slept beneath

101

it. I covered *that* piece of wood with other, smaller pieces of wood, such as the branches and twigs I had found. It all looked like the ribcage of some giant plant creature. Finally, I roofed the structure with pieces of foliage. There were several trees nearby, their leaves the size of dinner plates. They had a thick, leathery texture that felt durable enough to the touch.

It wasn't the impenetrable fortress I had wanted, but it would protect from rain and storms. To a degree. I have to say, once I had finished the whole thing, I was very pleased with myself. Had I a camera on my person, I would have documented the feat with photographic evidence. It wasn't flawless, but I felt a sense of achievement I hadn't encountered since the model aeroplanes of my youth.

I stood there and admired *my construction.* I grinned from ear to ear — even though there was nobody present to smile *at.*

* * *

After several weeks, I've concluded it's *quite nice here.*

The only major problem is the lack of other humans. I was never a fan of people, before — I only had an interest in the contents of their pockets. But a life without them seems rather awful. I hate to admit it, but I am lonely.

I've come to another conclusion as well, in a similar vein: I have to leave. Nobody is coming for me, I am sure. I don't know about the other passengers, but *I* am presumed dead. And even if — and that's a big *if* — they are searching for me, it's unlikely that they will find me. I depicted giant 'SOS' letters on the shoreline with rocks, but I've neither seen nor heard any planes or boats.

And so, I've resolved to leave my paradise. Oh, I know it

won't be easy, don't think I haven't pondered it and pondered it and pondered some more. I know they say to sit still in an emergency and wait for rescue. But it seems unlikely that rescue will ever come. And whilst I *could*, in theory, survive here for the foreseeable future, what then? What is there to life, besides living? I want to give love and receive love. My absence from society has instilled me with a long-forgotten fondness for my fellow man.

If I can build a shelter, I can build a boat.

Or, at the very least, something that doesn't sink.

* * *

As with the shelter, the raft took me several attempts.

The first few disintegrated upon contact with the waves. Several of my efforts dropped to the ocean floor rather fantastically. *Well*, I thought, *at least I've figured out how to make a good anchor.*

I made several failed experiments, each one better than the last. I learned which woods were sturdy *and* buoyant, and which of the vines made the strongest bindings. I figured out the best shape to build my raft, too.

I made a solid structural skeleton for the thing — much as I had for my shelter — with the strongest wood I could find. It was *bloody hard* to chop down with my self-made axe. I lashed together four columns and two rows. My foundation.

With bamboo shoots — sealed airtight with beeswax — I created two separate cylinders. They each had many bound tubes, every single one capable of flotation. I secured these cylinders between the columns on each side of the raft. I had something that looked a little bit like an 'H', only with two horizontal bars. It took me many, *many* attempts to realise that this form was the best I could manage. The water would flow down the centre, between the two buoyancy devices that would keep me afloat.

I also found a use for the thick green leaves that layered the forest's floor in the thousands. As a side note: I have become quite good at recycling; something I endeavour to do more of, should I make it back. I am ashamed to say I'd always been a bit wasteful, in my previous existence.

It took a lot of effort, but I've made something that — *at the very least* — will see me escape from the shore's greedy currents.

* * *

And so here I am, waist-deep in water.

I push my boat out into the open sea.

I've made a promise to myself if I ever make it back to civilisation alive. I am going to ask the receptionist, Gabby, out for a bite to eat. She forever asked me if I wanted to go for drinks, or have lunch, or go grab some coffee. I forever shook her off, with a lame excuse to boot. Well, no longer. Gabby, if you can hear me, *I'm on my way back, and lunch sounds lovely. How about 12, at the nice steak place down the road?*

Back in my older life, I had a mantra: *Perfection or nothing.* I have come to realise this was a bloody silly mantra to hold. I have since discarded it and washed my hands clean of its filth. I had pursued utter faultlessness, and it only brought me misery. I now think that perfection *does not exist*; we are either contented with what we have, or we are not.

Well, no longer. I will not strive for perfection. Instead, I will view the beauty of what I have. I will force myself to find the loveliness in the work that I do — even when others can't see it. I will seek to see perfection where it is not immediately obvious. I will marvel at the structures I make, even if they are not the sturdiest. Even if they collapse under a strong gust of wind. I will take pride in the boats I build, even if the planks of wood are not even. Even if water splashes up on board every other wave and soaks me to the bone. Even if my raft does not deliver me to safety, I will be proud of myself for having tried. Even if I die in the process.

If I do not try, I will be all alone on my beautiful island — for God knows how long. And that is not what I want. I seek that which for I yearn, even if all I want is to connect with other people on a level I had not done before.

I've made my boat, although I'm sure some would dispute that description. The logs are strong. The vines tying them are secure. I even have a sail, made from the offerings of the island's trees. I have no previous sailing experience, but I also didn't know how to build a shelter, either. I managed that, and so I will manage this. Or I won't. Either way, I have won.

Behind me, I can hear the call of the exotic bird. I glimpsed it, once, in all its splendour. I will not betray its trust by describing my feathery friend here. But if you are in the neighbourhood, take a peek — it's *gorgeous*. It is saying goodbye. *Goodbye and good luck.*

I've checked my sail and bound my belongings to the raft. It's going to be a rough journey, but I've set my mind to it. I suppose that's one of the better life lessons I've learned from my business career. I've made sure to pack backup logs and vines, should I need to do repairs along the way. I imagine I will. *Hope for the best, prepare for the worst*, isn't that what they always say?

The morning sun hasn't quite risen yet. The dark of the night has given way to gorgeous purple and pink lines that burn the sky in vivid stripes. The ocean water is cool and clear around my waist, as I carry my raft out from the shore. Small, friendly fish swim about me.

The sea looks calm at the moment, but I know looks can deceive, and I won't pretend that I'm in for smooth sailing. Nonetheless, I carry a lightness in my heart and a smile upon my face.

If I've learned nothing from this experience, at least I can say that I know how to build a boat.

It's the Count That Thoughts

T he vampire raised the blade, a mad grin on his face.
"And now for the feast!" His voice boomed through
the hall, carried across the air as if on the backs of
invisible bats. Outside, lightning lit the manor's grounds.
Thunder cracked the sky, the rumble of a grizzly bear's growl.
Somewhere deep in the bowels of the castle, a cathedral organ
played. The notes vibrated in their bellies, reverberated in their
bones.

He plunged the knife in. Those around the table made
appreciative noises. The count sliced bits off the cooked
carcass. He placed the slivers onto plates and passed them
around. Once the last of the guests had a serving, he poured
the drinks.

Red liquid, vital and bright, sloshed into crystal glasses. A
splash painted the vampire's pale complexion. He put his hand
in his mouth and sucked the juice away. "Mmm," he said,
"delicious!" A few of the guests grinned at each other.

Full plates in front, glasses of claret in hand, the vampire
raised a toast. "To family!" he said, chest puffed out. "To friends,
new and old! To trying new things and experiencing new ways
of life—" he raised his eyebrows at his children "—with an open
mind! And," he turned to a woman on his right and raised his

glass ever higher, "to love."

Everyone around the table raised their glasses. High. Triumphant. "To love!" they all cried, delirious smiles plastered over their countenances. Outside, the storm boomed once more. The organ rose in pitch, the notes morphed into something upbeat — yet discordant.

"And to my bride, the delightful Mrs Haversham."

"To Mrs Haversham!"

"To Mum!"

Deidre blushed. "Oh, please, stop it! Besides," she smiled at everyone around the table, from face to face, "I'm not Mrs Haversham any more."

"I was going to ask whether you were going to take his name or not," said Clara. "Mrs Lavode." She savoured the texture. "It's got a nice ring to it, doesn't it?" she asked her brother.

Deidre ushered them away with a wave of her hands. Her eyes twinkled. "No, no, I'm not Mrs Lavode!"

"Neither am I!" said the count. "Although, I never was, to begin with." That got a riotous round of laughter — the alcohol was already doing its job. "That is to say, I'm no longer Count Lavode." He smiled at Deidre. "Do you want to tell them, or shall I?"

Deidre turned to face her children — both biological and step. "We're now Mr and Mrs Haversham-Lavode!"

"Or, rather," interjected the vampire, "Count and Countess Haversham-Lavode!" That prompted a round of *oohs* and *ahhs* from the guests.

"Oh, how lovely!" said Elda. She was a young woman with a pale face and a long, slender neck. Her hair was pitch black, as were her nails.

"How modern!" said Dean. "Very twenty-first century, Mum.

Very cool of you, Mr— er, Count Lavode!"

Clara elbowed him in the ribs. "Haversham-Lavode!"

The vampire smiled at his step-children. "Please, call me Vincent." His smile dropped away. "Or Daddy."

Dean did a double-take. He glanced to his sister, his mother, back to the vampire. "I—"

Vincent burst into laughter, as did the other vampirically-inclined members of the party. "Oh, I'm only pulling your leg!" He let the laughter die down. He gestured at the plates. "Now, please, eat!"

The humans tucked into their turkey. They each paused, for a moment, as they bit into the meat. It was rather dry. They each shared a locked glance. Deidre willed her intention at her children with force. The message was loud and clear.

The vampires watched on with mild curiosity. They raised their chalices of blood to their lips and sipped. The actions were almost catlike. "Cheers—" Vincent looked to his wife "—that's how you say it, right? Cheers?" With confirmation, the vampire nodded and continued. "Cheers, my children. Drink. *Feast.*"

"Mmm, delicious," said Clara. "Right, Dean?"

"Mmf," said Dean through a mouthful of food. "Delifuth." His tastes had never been that refined. Deidre had always called him the family's walking garbage bin.

Clara cringed and looked away. She locked eyes with her step-father. "It's really good… Vincent." The name would become more normal with use.

"Oh, I'm so glad. We're not used to meals that require cooking, around these parts. Although, we do like to keep our finger on the pulse of society!" The Count burst into laughter, as did the older vampires. The younger ones grinned and rolled their eyes at their father. They exchanged a knowing look with their mortal counterparts. Embarrassment over parents transcended the barriers of life and death. And the living dead.

Dean nodded at his step-brother's glass. "How's the, um—" he swallowed his mouthful "—blood, Alphonse?"

"Delicious," said the vampire. His eyes sparkled like black coals. His hair, slicked to one side, was obsidian. He wore a three-piece suit. Blazer, waistcoat and shirt were all night-black. His tie was a deep crimson. Like Elda, he had black nails. Were they painted or was that their natural colour? Would it be rude to ask? "It's an excellent vintage, Father always has excellent taste."

Dean grinned and nodded. Was it allowed to ask where they got it? "I'm glad. It, er, looks great!" Had they killed him or her? Or milked them, like a cow? Dean's smile faltered. Which would be worse? Best not think about it. They were, after all, family.

"Oh, and I almost forgot!" Vincent pulled a cardboard box from beneath the table. "I've bought these." The vampire kept the box at an arm's length — as if he held a bomb. He read the words imprinted. "Christmas crackers." He raised an eyebrow and looked up at Deidre. A smile tugged at the corners of his lips, long fangs extended.

"Oh, Vinnie!" Deidre slapped the vampire on the arm. "You shouldn't have!"

The head vampire distributed the crackers amongst the party, human and vampire alike. The bloodsuckers rotated the cylindrical objects, this way and that. They raised it to their ears and shook it, listened to the rattle within. "Is it a bomb?" asked the Count's daughter.

"No, it must be bones. I know that noise." The young vampire waggled it. Alphonse nodded. "Small bones. Perhaps of a mouse?"

"No, see?" Clara demonstrated with her brother. "You each hold an end like this, right? And you each—"

The bang startled the vampires. "It is a bomb!" said Elda.

"Duck!" said Alphonse.

Vincent wore a concerned expression on his countenance. He glanced at his wife, who smiled and patted his hand. "It's fine, dear." After that, the vampire seemed more reassured.

Clara won the cracker. "Look," she presented the innards to the table, "it's fun." She unravelled her coloured paper hat — gold on one side, purple on the other — and pushed it down onto her head. The vampires squinted at her.

She fished a Fortune Teller Miracle Fish out of the cracker. "What's *that?*" asked the vampire's daughter.

"Oh, just a fortune-telling fish."

"Fortune?" asked the son. His eyebrows, stark black against his pale complexion, raised.

Dean grinned. "It's not *really* a fortune-telling fish. It's just a toy." Then he added: "For kids."

"You let children play with fortune-telling devices?" asked Elda. "Isn't that dangerous?" She shook her head. "You think you know humans…"

"Tell the joke," whispered Dean. "I think we've confused them."

Clara pulled the joke out and cleared her throat. "What do sprinters eat before a race?" She looked from face to face, eyes locked. The vampires looked at her, as if undecided whether she had lost her marbles. "Nothing," she said, "they fast!"

Dean slapped his forehead. "Oh Jesus, that was terrible."

The vampires said nothing. Clara repeated the punchline. "They *fast*." One second. Two. Three. Four. Five. Realisation dawned on Elda's face and she burst into laughter. She slapped the table as she giggled. Her father followed soon after.

Alphonse looked to his family with a confused grin. "I don't get it."

"Never mind, dear," said Deidre, "those jokes are always terrible. I think that's the point." She gestured at their crackers. "Now, pull yours!"

Seven minutes later, they all wore their paper hats — a gathering of kings and queens. They told their jokes and laughed until the tears streamed down their face. They howled without irony, their humour still in its infancy. They even giggled at the small *pop!* from the crackers — now that they knew it wasn't an explosive device.

Each pulled a terrible toy from the pried-open ribcages of the cylindrical cardboard. Marbles, plastic combs, puzzles and brainteasers, inexplicable oversized paperclips, and so on. The vampires grinned at the toys, pointed and laughed at each other with their hats on, pulled goofy faces. The humans, who'd danced this dance before, grinned along with them. The vampires' discovery of their tradition lit a warm fire in their hearts.

Outside, lightning illuminated the manor's grounds, lit up the place like fairy lights. Thunder cracked the sky, the chortle of a fat man in a red suit. Somewhere deep in the bowels of the castle, a cathedral organ played — a holiday song the humans all knew. It was close enough for them all to recognise and hum along. The notes vibrated in their bellies, reverberated in their bones.

The laughter echoed across the hall. It bounced through the

air like the dance of snowflakes.

Maledictions and Muffins

The witch waved her wand and whispered the ancient incantations.

The words snaked out of her lips, like a worm from an apple. Her opponent began to expand — growing, widening, *fattening*. It wouldn't be long until the object of her spellcasting bid *adieu* to this mortal world and exploded. Its insides would splatter in every direction.

But Mavis wasn't going to let them give up that easily, oh *no*. She had much more in store for the half a dozen targets. There would be quite a bit more magic they'd suffer before they could taste the sweet relief of death.

Ping! Her little timer went off. It was the face of a black cat with green eyes, the twisty dial in place of the nose. Mavis thought it was cute, but it hadn't impressed Jasper, despite her coos. He had turned his nose up at it and trotted away with a swish of his tail. He *still* wasn't a fan of his plastic counterpart. He eyed it as he approached. His mechanical, time-keeping brethren had informed him that treats would soon be available. If his keen nose hadn't told him already, of course.

"Oh, they're ready!" Mavis dropped her wand onto the flour-coated countertop — next to a dough-covered spoon. She slipped her hands into the oven gloves and pulled open the door. She basked in the heat that radiated from within. Her nostrils soaked up the delicious perfume of baked dough.

The witch slid the tray out and plopped it onto the heat-proof mat on the side. She shut the door behind her with a deft kick of her leg. Mavis had barely let go of the tray before Jasper wound his way around her ankles. He purred affection and begged for something good to eat.

I'm starving, those pleas seemed to say. *I haven't eaten in days. Look at me — I'm wasting away!*

"Get away, you chubby cat! You've had enough cakes to last a lifetime."

Jasper meowed at her. *What a rude thing to say! It's the fur, I tell you. I've got big fur.*

"I need to put you on a diet, Jasper. Your belly's almost touching the floor!" She shooed him away — not unkindly. "These aren't for you, Mummy's got to sell something for this shop to stay in business, hasn't she?"

Jasper grumbled as he trotted off, most likely in search of a sunbeam in which he could lounge and nap. *You never give me any food. I'm nothing but skin and bones...* Mavis grinned as she watched him go, and shook her head with affection. Once the hunter of biscuits and predator of treats was gone, she returned to her cupcakes.

Time for her favourite part of baking — the icing! In Mavis's opinion, the icing was so much more than an extra sweetness to the flavour, it was an *art*. She took great pride in the wonderful pieces she daubed across the tops of the glowing cakes. People came from miles around because they'd heard about her incredible treats by word of mouth.

As she often did when she got into a contemplative rhythm, Mavis began to sing the crooked rhyme of her elders. Albeit, with a culinary twist.

> *"Double, double taste and flavour,*
>   *Kitchen full of scents to savour.*
>   *Filling of a fruity cake,*
>   *In the oven rise and bake.*
>   *Pot of tea or warm eggnog,*
>   *Oft go well with chocolate log.*
>   *"Grab a fork!" your taste buds sing,*
>   *At the thought of pink frosting*
>   *On a cake of powerful colour,*
>   *Filled to brim with sugared butter.*
>
> *Double, double taste and flavour,*
>   *Kitchen full of scents to savour.*
>   *Wait 'til smells call back childhood,*
>   *Then the muffin's firm and good."*

Mavis brought her fresh wares to the glass case at the shop's front, where passers-by could glimpse them. One look, that was all it took. They'd hover for a moment, gazing at the array of cakes, all-but drooling down the fronts of their shirts. Once or twice, Mavis had heard the growl of a tummy, despite the pane of glass that separated them.

And then they'd come in, powerless to resist her magic. She reeled them in, a fisherman and his catch, a hook in their mouths. Often, they'd be unable to form full sentences. "How much?" they'd stammer and gesticulate at the smorgasbord of treats. "How much for the... the..." And then they'd trail off, eyes glazing over as they gazed at the glazed cakes. Mavis would smile and tell them the minuscule price. They'd hand over the change, their gaze never averted. Unaware when their coins bounced from the till and clattered to the floor. They would snatch the brown paper bag she gave them and gush their thanks and appraisals. If you'd overheard their praise, you'd think Mavis had saved a loved one from a fire.

Mavis undercharged for her wares; it was true. But, somehow, she couldn't bring herself to raise her prices. She wanted the world to know how good cakes tasted — everyone deserved something warm to bite into. Besides, the popularity of her shop alone was enough to keep her going. Between the hours of nine and five on any given weekday, Mavis' little bakery was *never* empty. *Ever*. There was always at least *one* customer inside — and often a great deal more.

The early morning sun now shone through the shop window. The smell of baked cakes was in the air, coupled with the irresistible aroma of brewed coffee. Mavis the witch wrapped her hands around her mug and took a sip. She sighed at the *rightness* of everything. Life was good.

She had a smile on her face, a song in her heart, a cup o' joe in her hands and cakes in her tummy — for quality control. The witch strolled over to her shop door and turned the key. *Click!* She flipped the sign around (*Come on in, we're open!*) and opened the door. The bell jingled overhead. The perfumes of her shop spilled out onto the street, where they would entice people to come inside. The bouquet of spring aromas rushed in and intermingled with the sweet delights.

The witch stood in the open doorway of her shop and sipped at her morning coffee. Soft brushes against her feet as Jasper purred about her and swished his tail. She closed her eyes and let the rays of sunshine fall across her upturned face.

The sign above the door said 'MAVIS' MALEDICTIONS AND MUFFINS', and beneath that: 'We'll put a spell on chew!'

Night Train to Pinea

"Tickets and passes, please! Tickets and passes!"

The bellow of the conductor startled John awake from his slumber. His eyes snapped open and he lifted his head from the table. Panic jolted into his veins like the crackle of electricity. His stomach lurched.

"Ticket?" John frowned and wiped the sleep from his eyes. "What ticket?" In his half-dozed state, the phrase came out as *Wha' tic'?*

"Tickets and passes, please! Tickets and passes!" The train conductor moved into view, he walked down the train carriage towards John. He was a portly fellow in a navy-blue uniform. There was a cap on his head and a thick moustache on his upper lip. His dark eyes twinkled with kindness. Once more, he echoed his request for tickets and passes.

John sat upright in his seat and looked around at his surroundings with confusion. "Where—" he began to ask, but then he caught the sight outside the window and the question died in his throat.

The evening sky was *purple*.

And not a *little bit* purple, but *purple* purple. John's eyes soaked in the colour and his jaw dropped down. He squinted at something in the distance. Was that a whale? *In the sky?*

Someone cleared their throat behind him. John twisted around from the hallucination to look at the train conductor. At least the man before him looked normal enough. A golden nametag on his breast declared the man to be Dorian May-Thompson. "Sorry to distract you from the lovely views, my dear chap, but I regrettably must ask to see your ticket. Or pass." He smiled at John. The expression was warm and soothed John immediately.

"Where... where *are we?*" asked John. He tried his best to keep the awe out of his voice. He also tried his best to not glance out of the window at the violet heavens and the oceanic goliaths. John didn't want to appear insane to the man. He could still see the vibrant colours, though — out of the corner of his eye.

"On a train, my dear chap," responded the conductor, matter-of-factly.

John gave in to temptation and stole a furtive look over his shoulder. Yep. The skies were still purple. And those things were whales. They flew closer, now. Three of them. John guessed they were a family. He rubbed his eyes and sighed. "I'm sorry, but..." John exhaled. "Could you please tell me what colour the skies are?"

"What colour the—" The conductor's eyes widened, and he chortled. It was a pleasant sound, somehow big and round. "What colour the *skies* are? Why, they're purple, of course!"

"They're purple. *Of course,*" parroted John. He looked back out the window. What was happening? "So—" John licked his lips "—*where* are we, exactly?"

"On a train?" Dorian's brow furrowed. The expression wasn't enough to rob him of his charm.

"Excuse me," John asked, in a more timid tone than he'd have liked, "but a train to *where?*"

Dorian's smile widened. "Why, to Pinea, of course!"

"Pin—" John shook his head. A thousand questions bustled up like bubbles in a fizzy drink. "I'm sorry, but *where on Earth is Pinea?*"

The conductor chuckled. "Ha! It's not, my boy!"

John was at a loss for words. "I'm sorry, I'm *very* confused. I've never been to Pinea. I don't know what it's like. I don't know anyone there. I don't know where it is. I don't—"

Dorian raised his hand. "It's your first time?" The conductor nodded, as if in answer to his question. And then, quietly: "Isn't this journey always the first time?" He seemed to have posed this riddle to himself because his eyes glazed over. After what felt like a minute of silence, John decided to interrupt the man's daydream.

"Um, excuse me? Mr., ah, May-Thompson? Sir?"

The conductor shook his head and waved away the vision. "Hm? What? Oh! Right, I'm sorry! Oh yes, yes, where was I?" Dorian raised a finger to his lips and tapped. "Yes, you've never been to Pinea. Of course you haven't. You're on this train, aren't you? People only *go* to Pinea, they never *return from* Pinea. So, if you're *here*, you've never been *there*, right?"

John was aware that his mouth hung open. Catching flies, as his grandmother used to put it. He shut it with a snap. "I don't follow, I'm afraid, Mr May-Thompson."

Dorian smiled at John. The smile contained an eternity's worth of wisdom, a universe's worth of knowledge. "Don't worry, my dear chap, you will understand in due time. Pinea is a lovely place, I've never heard a complaint about it. After all, there's a reason why nobody ever wants to leave, eh?"

"I'm still lost."

"Of course you are. But you won't be, fairly soon. Please trust me," said Dorian. "You might not understand now, but I do." The conductor placed a gentle hand on John's shoulder. His touch was soft. "*I do*. Everything will be okay, my dear fellow. You'll come to see that."

John nodded. He wanted to say, *If you say so*, but found that no words escaped his lips. A low squeak emanated from his voice box. He felt quite breathless.

The conductor removed his hand and raised his ticket machine. He tilted his head in a way that said, *Now, back to business, I'm afraid.* "Would you mind showing me your ticket? Only, I've got the entire train to get through, I'm sure you're aware."

John swallowed hard. There was a click in his throat. "I-I'm afraid I don't have a ticket to Pinea. I'm awfully sorry. I'm really sorry. In fact, I don't even know how I got on this train. Or *where* I got on it." And then after a pause, he added: "I'm very confused, I must admit."

The conductor waved the concern away, cheeks rosy under the light of the train carriage's lamps. "Let's have a look in your wallet, my friend. I'm sure you'll find a valid ticket in there. It's impossible to get on this train without one."

John got a distinct impression that the conductor wanted money. "How much is it?"

"Hm?"

"How much is it?"

"How much is what?"

"A ticket to Puh…"

"Pinea?"

"Yeah, that's the one."

"Nothing."

"Nothing?"

"Nothing."

"So why do you—"

"Let's just have a look," prodded Dorian. He wasn't unkind with his words or mannerisms, but he was firm in his insistence.

With neither the will nor the mental capacity to argue, John obeyed. He pulled the old brown wallet from his pocket and flipped it open on the table before him. "Look," he said to the conductor. "There's nothing here." John spread open the back pouch to reveal several crumpled notes. "I can pay you now if you'd like, but—"

"No, no money, my friend."

"Well, there's no ticket here. I'm sorry." John flicked through the few sections of the old leather to show its ticket-lessness. A picture of John with his arms around a smiling woman and a small girl flashed before their eyes.

The train conductor perked up. "Ah, yes! That'll do! Perfect."

"Huh?"

"*That.*"

John slid the picture out from behind its transparent plastic protection. "*This?*" He looked at the photo as if he saw it for the first time in his life. He'd had it in his wallet for as long as he could remember. It showed him with his arms around a woman and child on a sandy beach, the ocean behind burned by a bloody sunset. In the picture, John wore an open shirt and a straw hat askew on his head, and he had his eyes closed with laughter. The woman, who gazed at John with adoration, wore a flowing skirt adorned with bright patterns. The pigtailed little girl had a dripping icecream, which held her attention. The melted cream dribbled over her hands.

John remembered that day; there hadn't been a cloud in the sky. A gentle summer breeze had kissed their skin and dried them after their swim in the ocean. Yet, he didn't remember having a camera with him. Now that he thought about it, who had taken the picture? John frowned and leaned forward to get a closer look, but, before he could, Dorian spoke again.

"Great!" The conductor picked the photograph from John's fingers and clamped it into his machine. *Click-click!* "Thanks fella! Knew you had one on you, or else how else would you have gotten on to this train?" He then laughed at that, as if he'd told the funniest joke ever. The conductor dropped the photograph onto the table and moved on. He repeated his rallying cry for tickets and passes until a shut door quieted him.

John sat in stunned silence for a moment and let the bizarreness of the encounter soak in. He cocked one eyebrow and tilted his head to one side. A baffled puppy that tries to decipher an audio stimulus.

John glanced back out the window again, to verify the absurdities were still present. They were. Purple sky, flying whales. John nodded to himself, in acknowledgement of his fractured mind. He let his eyes roll over the scenery — the fields (at least *those* were the right colour), the hills, the grass, the clouds. When you ignored the oddness, it was quite beautiful.

When you ignored the oddness.

It was as John stared out the train window at the alien landscape that he became aware of something. John could see his reflection in the glass of the window. And in that reflection… something moved. Something on the table. In slow motion, like a character in a teen slasher movie, John turned his head to the table. The tendons in his neck creaked.

It was the photograph. Or, rather, the *people* within the photograph. They were *alive*.

Positive he was on the brink of a breakdown, John reached for the picture and picked it up. His hands trembled as he brought the photo up to his eyes. He realised his initial perception had been inaccurate. It wasn't *just* the people who moved. It was the entire *scene*.

John stared at the image. The air escaped his lungs, his heart *thrummed* in his chest like a hummingbird in a cage. A reflective grin grew on his face. The smile lit up his features and brought life to eyes that had previously seemed dull.

In the picture, the woman's mouth moved, but John couldn't make out the words. The look on her face and the glint of her eyes said everything. *I love you*. Her hair was windswept and *gorgeous*, and her pretty dress fluttered in the breeze. And in front, the child tried to lick her ice cream and catch the drips that fell before they plopped into the sand. The girl's eyes overflowed with giggling happiness.

And he, John, was laughing. He was laughing, he was laughing, *he was laughing*.

John gripped the photograph and closed his eyes.

Now that he thought about it, he could still feel the soft summer wind as it cooled his sunburned cheeks. Could feel the droplets of moisture in the air from the crests of the waves. Could feel the soft white sand — warm from the day's sunshine — silky smooth beneath his naked feet.

Somewhere, the seagulls flew overhead. They rode the warm updrafts and cried in the breeze. *Shhhhh*, said the ocean waves, *shhhhh*. *Everything will be okay, so just shhhhh. We've got everything from here, so shhhhh, my child, shhhh.* John could smell the beach's bouquet; sea air, saltwater, and sand. The rich smells of love. The aromas of life.

Distantly, *oh so distantly*, a voice over the speaker said, "Next stop, Pinea. Next stop, Pinea."

John slipped into the photograph, a boyish grin on his face. He let the scene take him.

Returning the Favour

"**D**on't panic," said the man with my face, "I'm not here to hurt you."

The words caught in my throat for a moment. My eyes traced his features. The shape of his head. The crook of his nose. The thickness of his lips. The colour of his eyes, the uneven brows, the off-centre teeth. He was me. He was me, he was me, *he was me*. But *I* was me. I was sure of it.

"I… " I looked over him once more. The man struck more than a passing resemblance to me. This was no doppelganger, no mere lookalike. This was a clone. An identical copy. If it weren't for the grey hair and wrinkles around the eyes and mouth, I would've sworn it was my mirror image. "How?" I didn't question his authenticity. You know you. You know you better than anyone else. Except for your mother and your lover. "How?"

"Time travel." He looked around. His head movements jerked. "But we don't have the time for this right now. The *how* isn't as important as the *why*."

I frowned and glanced back into the apartment. The New Year's Eve party was well underway. Charlotte hadn't seen me out on the balcony yet. *Either* of me. But it was only a matter of time. How would I explain it to her? Long lost twin? An older brother or another male relative? "Why are you here?"

"To save you." After a pause, he added: "Well, *technically* it's to save myself. If you don't survive the night, then I *certainly* won't. But I think you'll forgive my selfishness, won't you?" He said this last bit with a bit of a lopsided grin. How many times had I offered that very same smirk to friends and family?

"I'm in danger?" It sounded dumb even to my ears.

"You all are. *We* all are." He checked his watch. "We've got about 12 minutes until it starts."

"Until *what* starts?"

"I really don't have much time to explain, I'm afraid," he said. He then pulled a metal gun from his back pocket, only I'd never seen a gun like this in my entire life. It looked like something from space or one of those old sci-fi movies from the fifties. "Have you ever used one of these things before?" Before I could answer, he slapped himself on the head. "No, of course you haven't. *I* hadn't." He chuckled. "Sometimes I forget that you *were* me."

I looked at him. "I don't—"

He thrust the device into my hands. "It's a simple laser blaster. Point this end at the things you want to die — and believe me, you *will* want them dead — and pull this little fella to do the whole *pew-pew* bit."

I shook my head and tried to decline the weapon. "I'm sorry, but I don't know how to… I mean, I've *never*—"

"Jonathan," said Future Me, "you don't have a choice." He checked his watch again. "We've got less than ten minutes, now. If you don't fight, you die. And If *you* die, *I* die. And I'm not prepared to let that happen." He pushed the laser blaster into my hands. "Take the gun. Take it and use it."

I took the weapon. It was cold to the touch, and its weight

surprised me. I turned it over in my hands. There were pipes and tubes on the side, through which a fluorescent blue liquid pulsed. I admired the psychedelic colours.

A thought struck me. I spun around and searched the throng of people for Charlotte. Where was she?

A hand fell upon my shoulder. "Relax. I'm not the only one." A hand pointed. "See?"

I did. I saw Charlotte, my partner of seven years. My soon-to-be fiancée, if she said yes to the question I would pop when the New Year's countdown reached its finale. I could feel the bulge of the ring box in my back pocket, ever-present, *waiting*.

Charlotte was in conversation with another Charlotte. This second Charlotte was older, with a gorgeous grey streak in her hair and a few wrinkles on her pretty face. My heart thudded within my chest. Was this what she'd look like in god knows how many years? I thought she looked as beautiful as the day I met her, many moons ago.

"I know what you're thinking," said Future Me. "Because I thought the same thing that you did. But, please, calm down lover boy. Remember how little time we've got." As he said this, I saw Future Charlie pass my girlfriend an identical sci-fi gun. A second later, Charlotte spun around and her eyes scanned the crowd. It took me a moment to realise she searched for me. When our eyes locked, an unspoken understanding passed between us. "Charlie's telling her younger self the same thing I've just told you. Now, in about five minutes, *they'll* be arriving.

"Who are they?"

"You'll find out properly in due time, Jon. But for the time being, all you need to know is that they want all humans dead. Oh, and they're particularly aggressive. But, one thing they *aren't* is prepared. Prepared for *us*. They aren't prepared for *you* to be prepared. And that's what will be their death."

"And what about the others?" I watched my friends and acquaintances mill about the party. People laughed and chatted, drank and danced. Small talk between strangers. Big talk between old friends. "Do they live too? Why haven't any of their future selves come back to warn them?" I turned to Future Me. "Can *we* warn them? Can we save them?"

His eyes dropped to the floor. "Look… you'll learn more in due time. *Trust me*. For now, it's just us four. It will make sense in the future. *I promise*. I know it doesn't now because it didn't make sense back *then* to me, but—"

Inside, people began to chant. "TEN. NINE. EIGHT."

Future Me swore. "Lost track of time. Happens every damn time." Both Charlottes ran towards us with drawn weapons. A few people inside the party jumped out of their way, surprise and panic written across their faces.

"SEVEN. SIX. FIVE."

"Get ready," he said.

The balcony door burst open as Charlie and Future Charlie ran to us. "You boys ready?" asked Future Charlie, still as cool and calm as ever.

"FOUR."

"Ready, Hon," said Future Me.

"THREE."

"I love you."

"I love you too."

"TWO."

"I love you."

"I love you too."

"ONE."

* * *

We walked through the ruins of the party and checked the alien corpses littered across the floor.

"Pretty good for a man who's never used a laser blaster," said Future Me. "Nice shooting." The guns were still hot in our hands. The blue liquid bubbled at an accelerated pace, and I could feel the vibration. It was a good sensation. I thought I could get used to it. I supposed I would have to.

"If I recall," said Future Charlie, "you too were a dab hand at offing our intergalactic neighbours."

Future Me shrugged. "What can I say?" He smirked at Future Charlie. I watched the way that she blushed in response to his boyish grin. It was beautiful, but it was also spooky. *My* Charlie blushed in the same way when I said something goofy like that to her. I glanced over at Charlotte and was mildly jealous to see that she had red cheeks too. It was an odd feeling, to say the least.

"One thing I don't understand is," said Charlotte. "Why'd you come back at all?"

"I'm sorry?" asked Future Me with a frown, "I don't—"

"*I* know what she's getting at," said Future Charlie. "I had the very same question myself. What she's asking, husband dearest, is if *we're* here now, we obviously survived the encounter. The *initial* one, anyway. And if we survived, why come back in time to help our younger selves fight? If our younger forms are going to survive anyway, why not just leave them to it. Isn't that what you're asking?"

Charlotte nodded. "Yeah, that's pretty much it."

"Well, that's because something was lost, the first time. Only *I* survived. We come back to save Jonathan."

"I didn't survive?" I asked. My tongue and lips were numb.

"Not the first time, no. Sorry, sweetie."

"Oh," was all I could manage. The word escaped me like a winded sigh. I felt as if I'd received a gut punch.

"She came back for us." Future Me laid a hand on my shoulder. "That's the power of love, buddy." He glanced over to his wife. "From what I've heard, the first time was particularly difficult, when she did it by herself. Convincing both of us — both of *you* — to believe her. Convincing you to stand up and fight. After that, though, we've come back together. We do it together, always. It's much easier, now. Not *easy*, as you'll find out, but *easier*."

I nodded and glanced over to Charlotte. The bulge of the ring box throbbed in my pocket. "We're a team," I said, with a smile that she returned immediately.

Future Me smiled. "Exactly."

"Jonathan," said Future Charlie. "Don't you think we ought to...?"

Future Me checked his watch again. "Right you are, sweetie." He looked from me to my future fiancée. "Listen, guys, I'd love to chat with you all night, but it's taking a *lot* of power to send us back here. Every minute is expensive. Jon, my man, Charlie, my love... we've gotta boogie."

"How do we thank you?" I asked, at a loss for words.

"Surely there's something we can do for you guys?" asked Charlotte.

The husband and wife grinned at each other. "Don't worry about it," said Future Me. He put an arm around the woman who'd marry me. "You not dying is all I could ever ask for.

"And besides—" he shared a sideways glance with Future Charlie "—in a few years, you'll be returning the favour."

Routine

D aisy wakes me up each day with a kiss.
I always sleep longer than her, so she's always the
one to wake me up. I sometimes wonder how long
she's been up before she decides to rouse me — minutes, hours?
Does she get up to see the sunrise? She doesn't seem to mind,
though; she's all-smiles when I open my eyes.

She waits as I put on my slippers and throw on my dressing
gown. Daisy never hurries me — even though I'm bleary-eyed
and clumsy and fumble my way through the actions. Once
we're both up, we head down to the kitchen together. Our
footsteps pad against the carpeted stairs in unison.

In the kitchen, my first port of call is the kettle. I've heard
some start the day with neither a warm nor a caffeinated
beverage. I've made it my life's rule to avoid such people. I
don't trust someone who can be chatty and loud first thing —
especially before that first mug of coffee.

Well, that's not *completely* true. Daisy's a morning person,
through and through, and I trust her with my life. The
excitement emanates from her as we sit at the kitchen table.
It bubbles away inside her, like fizz in a carbonated drink.
She doesn't even need caffeine — nothing but crystal-clear
water for her, even first thing. No wonder her hair's luxurious.

But she knows I need time to adjust to the land of the living. Especially after my alarm rips me from the pillowed panoramas of Dreamland. She's never complained about me not being a morning person, and for that, I'll always love her. She accepts me as I am. The least I can do is return the favour. Daisy's the exception to the rule.

After the kettle's boiled, I brew the coffee. I inhale the aroma as the golden sunlight falls over my closed eyes. And then I get breakfast ready. It's become an unspoken rule in this household that *I'm* the one who's responsible for all culinary duties. I don't mind at all; in fact, I've come to love the routine. Daisy would like it to start a *bit* earlier — her tummy's growls could wake the neighbours — but she's never grumpy. Her positive energy is inextinguishable.

Once I've plated up our food, we sit at the kitchen table and enjoy our breakfast in silence. I sip at my coffee, Daisy sups at her cool water like there's no tomorrow. We each shovel down the delicious morsels. We don't need an exchange of words to fill the hush — we're content to be in each other's presence, as we sit and prepare for the day. We gaze into each other's eyes and grin — a mutual understanding between us without need for words.

After I've cleaned up the dishes from breakfast, I like to have a shower. I don't know why, but I need to shower every day, even if I'm already clean. Something about it wakes me up, and I can't start the day without a good scrub. Daisy thinks I'm crazy for showering every day. Her blonde locks are gorgeous, and washing more often than she does would strip her hair of its pretty sheen.

Once I've had my shower, Daisy and I head out for a little walk. I never used to go out for *just* a walk — I didn't see the point. But, at Daisy's insistence, it's become something that I've done more and more. She's very active, and her energy has rubbed off on me. I've started to love our morning walks together. The gentle breeze that rustles the tree leaves. The soporific sunshine that warms the skin. The companionable silence between two good friends.

Unfortunately, after our morning stroll, I have to go to work. Adulthood, right? Sometimes it can be a slog, but we do what we have to do to make ends meet. I don't hate my job, but I don't love it either. I know many think your job is the most important thing, but people are so much more than their work. Who cares if you work in a bank or a coffee shop? Who cares if someone makes over 100,000 a year or minimum wage? Provided they have enough to live. All that matters to me is if someone is kind, warm, welcoming and friendly. And — for the record — Daisy is the nicest soul I've ever had the pleasure to meet.

Daisy lazes around the house all day. Sometimes she lounges on the sofa. Other days, she relaxes in the garden — basks in the sunshine and smells the pretty aroma of the flowers. The daisies are her favourite — and not because they're her namesake. I don't mind at *all*, and she seems happy enough. If my job means she can have a comfortable life, then it's all worth it. She's satisfied in not doing much, and I'm in awe of that. Daisy takes enjoyment from sheer *existence*, she loves each moment for the fact that it's *here*. I'm sure there's a wealth of knowledge she could pass on to the monks in Tibet.

The worst part about going to work — by a country *mile* — is having to leave Daisy for several hours. I hate it and she hates it. A fact she makes all too clear to me, every time I'm about to step out that front door. She comes and gives me a hug and a kiss — kind acts of affection to make the departure all that much more difficult.

Daisy's always there when I come home after a long day. Or a short day. A tough day. Or an easy day. It's all the same to her, as long as I come back at the end of it. And to see her smile, her eyes full of love — it makes the baggage of the day fall away as I cross the threshold.

Before I've even managed to change into my jeans and t-shirt, Daisy tries to drag me outside. Even if I'm exhausted from the day, I always give in. Who could say no to her? The twinkle in her eyes? Her constant grin? I know I couldn't, and I'm not sure I'd like to spend much time around anyone who *could*. Besides, even if I *am* dog-tired, I'm always glad to get out of the house and do some exercise. Fresh air blows the cobwebs in your mind away. A stroll at the end of the day makes it *that bit* easier to relax.

When we get back, as the sun drops below the horizon and burns the sky pink and orange, our first mission is to make a cup of tea. With a fresh mug in hand, I get our food ready for the evening.

Our evening meals together are a mirror image of breakfast. Daisy and I sit at the kitchen table and enjoy our food in a companionable hush. After we've finished our meals — with lots of noise and mess — I clean up before we head to the lounge for a cuddle on the sofa.

Daisy doesn't mind what we watch on television. Neither do I. I like comedies and upbeat programmes — the ones that make you laugh, the ones that make you smile. Daisy likes whatever I like. She's very easy going, as far as entertainment goes.

And as far as life goes, for that matter.

When either one of us starts to yawn — they say it's contagious — I switch the T.V. off and we head upstairs to bed. Our feet pad against the carpeted stairs in unison.

I brush my teeth, tell Daisy I love her, and turn off the light. I drift off to sleep in my tranquillity. I used to have insomnia, but Daisy turned out to be the cure. I'm not sure if it's the general improved happiness or increased exercise that's done the trick. Perhaps it's the genuine affection from another living being — pure, unconditional love. That might have been the ticket.

Sunrise, sunset. Life with Daisy is happy and colourful. It's not always good weather outside, but Daisy provides enough sunshine for the world. It's true what they say about man's best friend.

The world would be a much better place if more people acted like dogs.

Sea the Moon

he seagulls wept.

They had woken her from her sleep. It was funny, now that she thought about it. She'd also listened to their shrill pleas as she drifted off. It reminded her of the song her mother had sung to her as a baby.

Sunset and sunrise, bird calls and bird cries.

Simone rolled out of her bed and the tidal swell of the world rolled beneath her feet. *Circles and orbs, circles and orbs.* She wobbled over to the window on legs made of string. *It's all just circles and orbs. Or spheres. Is 'spheres' the word I'm looking for?* She rested her elbows on the windowsill and cradled her chin in the cup of her palms. Her glazed eyes gazed outward. What Simone saw on the surface of the midnight ocean confirmed her notion that it *was* all circles and orbs. Or spheres. Perhaps 'spheres' is a better word.

The moon, fat and full, bobbed up and down on the ink-black waves. Higher and then lower it dipped and nodded, in lethargic motions. It was soporific. The sea was almost impossible to see. If it wasn't for the white foam that bubbled at the tips of the waves, Simone wouldn't have been able to tell it was there *at all*. Well, by *sight*, anyway. She could smell the salt in the air through the open window. And the seagulls continued to plead, of course.

Hush, said the waves. *Hush; roll with us. Hush now, child. See the moon, soak it in. Hush, hush, hush.* The sand beneath her naked feet was cool and damp. The sensation was rather nice. The wet beach against her bare skin was smooth and silky. It reminded her of the poem her father had told her when she was a little girl.

Sunrise and sunset, soil rich and shoreline wet.

The moon *bob-bob-bobbed* in the currents. They said that the moon didn't glow — it reflected the sun's light. But to look at it now, and the illumination that shimmered from it, Simone knew this to be false. *Of course* the moon glowed. Look at it. And who, pray tell, were 'they'? *Circles and orbs, spheres, o' spheres.*

Alone on the stretch of coast. As far as the eye could see. As far as the ear could hear. As far as the soul could search. As far as the heart could feel. Simone walked on, toes in the saturated silt. She was aware of her home and her sanctuary, somewhere off to her right, further inland. Or was it over to the left, somewhere in the ocean? Perhaps it hid behind the pregnant moon? Her bed called to her, to the land of sleep, the cloud of dreams. Her cosy little hidey-hole, with her pot of tea and her lit incense. But she resisted. And she walked on.

The familiar sadness flowed into her, from sources unknown. There was a great celestial jug above her. An inky, silky trickle of liquid dribbled from the spout into the soul. And so, to counteract this stream of grief, Simone threw herself into a somersault. Right there on the shoreline. Her hands dug into the soggy sand. If the melancholy would fill her, well, then she'd pour it back out again, wouldn't she? Besides, even if she were unsuccessful, nobody could be unhappy in a somersault. *Nobody.* It reminded her of a quote from the book her grandfather had given her as an adolescent.

Moon up and moon down, a smile's just an upturned frown.

Simone landed with deft and her soft nightgown billowed about her. Her mother might've chastised her indecency. But there was nobody except the moon to witness such impropriety. *Circles, orbs, spheres and spheres.* She laughed at the thought and broke out into a run — her heels carved divots in the beach. She clapped her hands together to rid them of the sand that clung like a glove. The sound reverberated across the cove. It bounced back to meet her — a percussive orchestra that faded away into the whisper of the waves.

In circles, she walked, in orbit around the sea. Overhead, the stars glittered. In the ocean behind, the moon reclined on the waves. High above, the seagulls continued to weep and plead and sing their miseries into the breeze. Simone pondered how easy it would be to go mad in the relentlessness of reality. The rigid conformities. The cuboid skeletons into which we force our fragile human minds. Round, squishy and delicate. It reminded her of the words her grandmother had spoken, the day she died.

Moon full and moon wanes; awake we're mad, asleep we're sane.

If this was reality, Simone couldn't wait to fall asleep. *And if this is a dream?* her mind asked. "Well, then I never want to wake up," she told the waves that shushed, the gulls that pled. "The only time I'm happy is when I dream. I wish I could dream forever."

As the last syllable dropped from her lips like a dewdrop from a blade of grass, the blanket of her bed enveloped her. Simone couldn't remember the walk home, but then again, wasn't that always the case?

The pot of tea steeped on her nightstand. Trails of steam rose to destinations unknown — perhaps to the ceiling, perhaps beyond. Simone poured herself a mug and relished the gentle *slosh* as it splashed against the ceramic. Somewhere, her incense burned. The smell was warm and rich; somehow cosy. The spicy aroma made her bedroom seem smaller. It made her feel safe, soft, and warm.

Simone took a sip and emptied her cup. The soft liquid trickled down into her, filled her to the brim, heated her from within. Her eyelids started to droop, so she placed the mug on the side table before sleep could steal her away. As she let her head drop to her pillow, a stone into a pond, she took one last glance at her open window. The curtains billowed in the breeze.

The moon was fat and full and happy. And it *glowed.* Illuminations shimmered through the onyx waves.

And now...

Now, the seagulls wept again.

Sunset and sunrise, bird calls and bird cries.

snoitseuQ and srewsnA

"**B**ecause we're here."

The words hovered in the space between them for a moment. From the mind of one and into the ears and heart and soul of the other.

The Questioner took the answer in all seriousness. On the surface, it seemed like a flippant, *careless* answer to what had been an earnest question. But the Questioner knew better. The answer, although simple, contained a lifetime's worth of wisdom. Presented in its most basic building blocks by the Answerer. Succinct. Simple.

Overhead, a seagull cawed its melancholic love song to the ocean waves. The Questioner observed as it flapped its wings and glided on an updraft of warm air. It travelled in a manner that humans would never experience. The pair watched the bird, lonely and alive, as it flew across the heavens. They tracked its movement, oblivious to its decreased pace.

But the bird didn't slow *itself* down. It neither descended to land nor met resistance in a headwind. No, this was something else. Something completely unprecedented. Neither one noticed the bird slow down. They were subject to the same anomalous blip in the otherwise steady course of time and space.

Everything around the two persons by the ocean's edge began to grind to a halt. As if the very rotation of the Earth itself decelerated by friction. It spun on its axis within a pool of treacle. Its inner gears trundled, grumbled, *clunk-clunk-clunked* at a lesser and lesser pace, until...

Time stopped with a mechanical thud. It echoed through the very core of existence itself and resounded in every living thing.

The seagull hung motionless, its white wings mid-flap, its cries silenced by time's lack of passage. The ocean's waves paused mid-break, specks of foam suspended in the air. The Questioner and the Answerer sat in the sand, side by side, content in each other's presence. A frozen sea breeze ruffled their hair and clothes. Strands of blonde and brunette pointed away at odd angles as if gelled for some bizarre new trend. Their clothes — shirts, jackets, trouser legs — appeared starched, caught mid-flutter.

Not a sound was audible. The air molecules necessary for the conduction of auditory vibrations were locked in place. That light remained was a curiosity within a curiosity, an anomaly within an anomaly. Surely, the spectrum of light cannot exist without time, *can it?* And yet, here we are.

The sight was something eerie — if there had been anything able to see it. Everything was *too* still. It was *stiller* than still, stiller than *death*. To say that the scene looked like a photograph would be half right. Yes, all was motionless. Yes, the picture *looked* nice. A sandy beach. A grandparent and a grandchild sat by the water's edge. Moody waves crashed in front of them. A bird flew above through the grey and cloudy sky. And yet, something lacked that would have been detectable in a photograph.

143

The *aliveness* still images capture was absent.

It's hard to say for how long, exactly, the scene remained paused, for time itself was no longer in motion. Perhaps it was for a second or two, perhaps it was closer to eternity. Maybe it was the length of time it takes for a kettle to boil and a pot of tea to steep, or perhaps it was the length of a movie. Maybe it never even paused at all, and only *appeared* to have halted. An illusion, of sorts, due to the perturbation of its inner workings. Regardless, the slowdown *of* time and the perceived pause *in* time were not the ends of that day's oddities.

Something curious began to happen.

Or, rather, something curious *continued* to happen.

Knulc-knulc-knulc. The Earth began to spin again. Its inner cogs once more groaned with their grinding workload. *Knulc-knulc-knulc.* But the internal sound — more of a *sensation* than an actual noise — was not the same as before. It went in the *other* direction. It distorted and wobbled like a rewound cassette tape.

Knulc-knulc-knulc, knulc-knulc-knulc. The backtracking sped up, the change now visible. The figures and the world moved once more — a mirror image of the actions they'd taken not too long ago.

The seagull cried its alien, backwards cry and it *flap-flap-flapped* its wings. It moved in reverse and retraced the course it had taken across the sky moments earlier. The ocean's waves spun away from the shore, ejected out by the dark, damp sand. The swirled waters and flecks of foam retreated and rose. They joined the rollers that sank into swells and faded away from the beach. The wind sucked rearward, as if from a vacuum. It stroked and swept hair and cloth and sand in the same fashion as it had done when it travelled forwards.

".ereh er'ew esuaceB" unsaid the Answerer. Not *unsaid* as in it wasn't spoken, *unsaid* as in the spoken words reversed. They slurped back up into the mouth of the Answerer like a noodle of spaghetti. A second after, their mouth closed and the words travelled back down. Down their throat and into that place that speech originates from.

Next came the pause that had preceded the answer. It wasn't very long, but it was thoughtful, and this reflected in the Answerer's face. The wizened countenance exhibited all the notions of intense thought. In the opposite direction. From the arrival of the answer to the contemplation to the reaction. And, finally, to the moment at which they listened to the Questioner pose their thought.

The question was then sucked back up into the mouth of the Questioner. It retained the childlike honesty in those wobbled, distorted syllables. Despite how jumbled they sounded.

Unlike the reversal — which had slowed, stopped, and rewound — time's resumption was immediate. Like a paused video *unpaused* for playback once more. The universe's tension released — an elastic band pulled backwards.

The Questioner loosed their question, in all its urgency and unshielded ignorance. From grandchild to grandparent. That age-old ponder about life and existence. That question asked by every human once they reach an understanding of themselves. That inquisition from every person when they *demand* to know the universe.

"Why are we here?"

The Lonely Earth

She stepped barefoot onto the grass, the night damp against her skin.

She breathed in and relished the fresh air. It cooled her throat and lungs — delicious. The aromas of the evening danced on her tongue. A chilly breeze, wet grass, darkness. It was strange to say darkness had a taste, but it did. She would be the first to argue so, even if she couldn't quite articulate what she meant.

She sighed and craned her neck to look at the night sky. The stars glinted down at her, like faerie lights glued to a giant dome. They twinkled, somehow *close* despite their distance. Cosy, almost. Tranquil and calm. And around those pots of gold and silver speckled across the heavens, the night was inky black. A juxtaposition with the bright glow of the cosmic vista. The blackness of the night looked thick and sticky, like tar. She knew that wasn't the case, knew the blackness was a void, a vacuum. And yet, she felt it in her soul that the blackness was full — palpable. As if she could reach out and plunge her hand into its endless waters. She imagined the reflective obsidian liquid as it coated her fingers.

The night was silent, the night was alive. There were no sounds, yet nature's orchestra played its nocturnal symphony.

The wind hushed through the trees and the bushes and the blades of grass. The crickets *chirp-chirp-chirped* to themselves and anyone who'd listen. A sound she'd always found comforting. A sound of home, a sound of peace, a sound of isolation, a sound of solitude, a sound of acceptance. And the stars overhead seemed to sing to her, too. Not an audible sound — she'd admit she might have gone crazy if there was — but a pressure, a *presence.* It bore down on her, pushed like the weight of a thick blanket on a winter's night. A vibration, a drone, the flutter of a hummingbird's wings, the palpitations of an enraptured heart. It was there if you opened yourself up to it.

She breathed in again and relished the rich bouquet of flavours and smells. Body and mind dropped down from a state of high anxiety to a low level of acceptance. She fought nothing, she railed against nothing. She *flowed*, a luminescent jellyfish on the infinite tide of the midnight ocean. The graceful waves of the endless waters were deep and dark and cool and refreshing. Her glow faded into the brine and trickled away from her. It faded with distance. She let go of everything — those grating, churning, buzzing chatters of worldly worries. "Take it, drop it in the ocean," her mother had told her. "Watch as it falls into nothingness, leaving you behind."

Her heart became weightless. It first rose in her chest, like a balloon in the fist of the little girl she'd been, and then left her body. It soared and flew. Euphoric. Her hopes and dreams swirled and around her in silken ribbons — everything possible. That childlike magic returned to her once more, an emotion that was hers. An enchantment. It had drifted away through the grey humdrum. Through the endless beat and churn of civilisation's mechanical heart. She'd never let it go again, she swore to herself. *Promised* herself. She had it once more and she craved it. It was cool water after stumbling through the desert. Perfect and chilly, quenching and *good*, dark and endless, a drop in the ocean, a plunge into the depths.

She was a baby. She was elderly. She'd been born yesterday. She'd just died. She was all these things and none of these things. She felt eternity stretch out before her in all directions. She was a speck of dust. She was everything.

The words rose from her heart and bubbled to the surface of her still inner waters. At first, they were nothing but a blurred smoothness. But as they got higher and higher they took shape. They formed and twisted, their material was malleable. Before she knew it, the words erupted from her lips, urgent and honest. A desire to know, a *need* to know.

She asked a question. *The* question.

A question on the day of her birth, before she learned the shape and size and the colour of words. Before she'd received the bias of language.

A question on the eve of her death, once she'd learned all she would ever learn within the reaches of her mind.

She asked it every morning of her life, as the sun flamed into the sky, red and orange. She asked it when she didn't even know she asked it. She pushed it aside in favour of mundane hubbub, the emptiness too great for her thoughts to bear.

She asked it every evening, as night's tendrils swept over the horizon and the stars twinkled. She asked it consciously, as she stared at the night sky. Her mind chewed it over. Tossed it this way and that. Looked at it from every angle and under every light. The vastness of the possibilities was so great, so magical, so *wonderful*.

It was a question to which she had no answer, and yet she

still asked despite the silence that followed. The silence that *screamed*. It was a question she would never have a response to. She'd know the answer when she died. She'd know the answer before she was born.

Her heart rolled in her chest, a ship over an ocean wave.

She asked the question to the night sky. Her words formed a cloud of vapour that drifted from her parted lips.

"Are we alone?"

The Things That Do Not Float

Shaun jumped from the cliff's edge.

With each second, he felt the temperature drop and the pressure rise. The sensation of the movement was faint; if he closed his eyes, it felt as if he didn't move at all.

Down and down he went. He fell forever.

"Do you have to?" his mum had asked.

He dropped, he was dropping, he would continue to drop. Always, always.

"Would you like me to come with you?" his dad had asked.

Further and further he coasted away from the world above and behind him.

"I don't know why you're bothering, it's all gone now, anyway," his sister had said.

Shaun glanced up — for a moment — and realised he could no longer see the precipice from which he had leapt.

"Yes. No. Because I have to," he had replied.

The light changed. The world around him shifted through hues of blue. From a bright azure that sparkled to the grey-black cerulean that pressed upon him from all sides. He flicked on his Aqualite and a broad beam exploded from the cylinder clipped to his shoulder. It revealed a face where before there had only been a shadow.

Shaun screamed. And then he remembered the regulator clamped in his mouth. He inhaled a small sip of the brine. Not enough to cause him to cough, but enough to make him wince from the taste. The illuminated face looked surprised, and turned and darted away. It retreated into the safety of the distant gloom that the light didn't penetrate.

Shaun continued his descent. His heart ricocheted within his chest. In the gigantic silence of the depths, the blood throbbed in his ears like the bass thump of a nightclub.

Shaun had come of age and was thus allowed to Go Down. His parents could not stop him as they had throughout his younger years. *Eighteen years old and dropping into the abyss*, thought the young man. But this was what he had wanted for as long as he could remember. Shaun wondered, now that he had it, did he *want* it? Or had he only wanted this because he couldn't have it? Now he was free to do so, would he do this again, or would the one time be enough? Would he return older and wiser? Would he understand why almost nobody ever decided to Go Down? Would this journey strip him of his youthful dreams and ambitions?

Questions, questions, and questions floated around his head. Like the very bubbles he exhaled. Unlike the pockets of air, the naggings in his mind didn't float off, upwards — destined for release.

Shaun fell into the darkness.

* * *

Shaun was close now.

For several minutes he had been able to see the silhouettes of skyscrapers in the distance. Too far away for details. But their ominous shadows could be nothing but those human con-structions. At least, Shaun hoped. He pushed the nightmarish ideas and visions of monsters away. *Childish thoughts, childish thoughts*, Shaun chastised himself, *you're better than that. You're old enough, now. If they knew you got scared, they'd smile smugly and tell you, "See? We told you so!" No. No.*

Beneath him was an inky pool of blackness. It stretched from the ragged cliff-face behind him to the far reaches of his vision. The sheer and utter *nothingness* made his stomach turn. Shaun had never been afraid of water, but he felt a vertiginous sense of thalassophobia.

Besides the Aqualite strapped to his shoulder, Shaun also had a Light Cannon secured to his belt. It was a bit bigger than the Aqualite and looked like a gun. He unclipped it now and clicked it on. A sister beam to the Aqualite's ray of brightness shot out from the end of the Light Cannon. Shaun directed the light stream from the Cannon downwards.

The beam was not strong enough to light all that was below, but Shaun saw enough. Rooftops, streets, what had once been above-ground gardens and parks. Schools of silvery and multicoloured fish teemed in giant orbs of thousands. Sharks — hammerheads, threshers, and mackerels — patrolled the city skyline of old. The sight of the predators made Shaun's heart-rate speed up. But for the time being, they seemed uninterested in this human's invasion.

What had been a bustling metropolis was *still* a bustling metropolis — but for aquatic life.

Shaun dropped down the edge of the cliff-face. The left-behind world loomed up to greet him, like an old friend. *Welcome back, Shaun,* said that watery cityscape, *it's been too long. We've missed you.*

* * *

He unattached himself from the Lifeline.

Shaun knew he wasn't supposed to — but he had to. He had to look. He had to see. He had to live it, feel it, and breathe it; not with his lungs, but with his heart.

His feet had hit the inundated floor of the street with a dampened thud minutes earlier. His heart seemed to have echoed the sound — it reverberated from his very core to the world around him.

Ka-thunk! He let go of the Lifeline and let it dangle. It swayed and danced in a gentle current. *Is there an alarm blaring, up there?* Shaun thought. *Do they know I've severed the Lifeline?* They did, right? It was his safe connection to the above. Both a rope that led the way home and a provider of oxygen should his tank run out or fail. Shaun observed the snakelike movements of the heavy-duty tube. No bubbles escaped its mouth.

Shaun shrugged. Why worry now? It was a problem for him when he returned to the surface. *If* he returned to the surface.

Shaun set off at a stroll. He moved in exaggerated slow motion. Like the astronauts in that grainy black and white video from Tranquility Base.

The Lifeline behind him waved like a flag in the breeze.

* * *

The entirety of the city's tenants had departed, and aliens were the new occupants.

Shaun walked the urban streets and tried to take it all in. He'd need a decade to document the sights of the new conurbation. He meandered in a vague approximation of the route he needed

153

to take. He let himself wander here and there. He followed wherever his overwhelmed senses directed him.

The buildings had eroded into rounded shapes, their sharp corners now softened. The metal had rusted, flaked, and browned. Most of the glass was gone — either broken by the environment or by deep-sea denizens. The road beneath his feet had cracked and peeled — here and there entire chunks of paving were missing. But Shaun did not have many issues traversing these little obstacles. When he came across a gap in his path, Shaun used underwater physics to his advantage. He swim-jumped over, like a character from a videogame.

Multicoloured corals sprung up all over this artificial reef of concrete and steel. He approached a crossroads — one he *remembered* from before. On his right, before the two roads intersected, a wall of yellows, pinks, purples, and greens rose. Flat plants that looked like cousins of desert succulents. They piled on top of each other, grew over one another, content with the blurred boundaries. *They look like a cosy family*, thought Shaun. The location had once been a city bank. Large and marbled, the smell of freshly-cleaned carpets ever-present. Shaun considered the new additions as a great improvement.

To his left, thin reedy plants swayed in the abyssal breeze — a mass of a thousand shades of green. Fish darted in and out of the seaweed's maze, ignoring the extra-terrestrial in their midst.

Beyond the intersection, there had been a small inner-city park. Detached from reality, Shaun crossed the roads and entered the reformed gardens. He passed through the long-gone gate, eyes on stalks.

The trees had rotted under the water. Their lifeless husks supported new organic structures. Staghorn corals of oranges and blues. Tabulate corals of salmon pink. A thousand more, which spanned the entire colour spectrum, sprouted up where once had been elm and oak.

Fish — so many he couldn't name half of them — whirled and dashed in a million directions. Some were yellow with blue stripes. Others were orange. Some were pink on top and white on the bottom. Others were the same blue as the waters, which made them all but invisible.

Bioluminescent plankton flashed — pink, red, purple, blue — in the dim recesses of the park. They lit his way in an all-natural firework display. Had he not gripped the regulator between his teeth, his mouth would have been agape in awe. He switched off his lights and walked through the gardens aided by the light of a billion organisms.

Shaun passed through the city common in a daze. He came out the other side, like a man who wakes from a dream.

Not far, now.

His stomach churned and twisted.

* * *

After five minutes, Shaun laid eyes upon what he had come down here to find.

At first, he didn't recognise it, and why should he have? It had undergone the same change as the rest of the megalopolis. Nature had not spared it, for it was not special — at least, not to the ocean.

His family home (*the old family home, Shaun, the old one*) used to sit in the middle of a row of identical houses. The house hadn't moved — if you ignored the fact it was now leagues under the sea. It still sat in the middle of the row.

155

But the houses were no longer identical. *Mother nature*, thought Shaun, *the original hipster.* The ocean had uniquely decorated each house. Corals, plants, and seaweeds now bloomed throughout the neighbourhood. Each one a different colour and shape.

Shaun's heart beat hard. It felt as if the blood-pumping organ was at the base of his throat. He stepped towards the door, which was still in one piece. The number plaque — *3317* — had rusted but was legible. He ran his fingers over the numbers. Small flakes of rust drifted away. Feeling like a spaceman, he lifted his hand to the handle. For a brief moment, he worried the damn thing wouldn't open.

Yet he needn't have panicked, as the seawater had corroded the latch. *And* the hinges. Shaun turned the handle and pulled, and the entire door came free from its frame. He staggered away as the thing fell forwards and came to a gentle rest face-down on the floor. Shaun had to suppress a giggle — laughing was hard with a regulator in your mouth.

Like Neil Armstrong, Shaun took a giant step and entered his old house.

And discovered it was no longer his.

Inside, shafts of light broke up the darkness. They shot at odd angles. Algae and barnacles scaled the walls, and waist-high sea reeds grew from the floors. He glanced left and right — into the shadows of the dining room and the living room. He decided to not tarnish his memory of those happy places.

He went up the stairs and took care to not disturb the small biosphere that bloomed there. All around, life *thrived*.

His bedroom was not what it had been. The window was gone, and aquatic vegetation had invaded. The television was a ruined skeleton, and what sat beneath it must've once been a games console. Shelled crustaceans now smothered it. His bed was a tangle of purple and green vines that writhed. His wardrobe now homed an eel — which frightened him before it disappeared into a hole in the floor.

Shelves of toys. Blanket forts. Cartoons and comics. Stuffed animals, soft carpets. Colourful nightlights. A view of the street below, where the children rode bikes and kicked footballs and played and laughed.

The vision of his old hideaway started to rip.

He looked at it all; the things that had not floated away. It was not evidence of the child he had been, it was an echo, a sketch, an outline, a shadow. Fading, *fading*.

It hit him in the gut — everything, all at once.

Shaun remembered.

* * *

They abandoned everything when The Great Rise claimed three-quarters of the land.

Shaun had been a child, no older than six. He remembered the *before* times — both good and bad, for one cannot exist without the other. He remembered the event itself. The incessant talks of the *grown-ups*, the endless debates. The initial ambivalence that turned into a mass panic.

Before, thought the boy. *Before*, thought the man. *Before*, thought Shaun. *Before*.

He clung to gold, faded memories. Greenness, grass, and trees. A cool breeze. The tinkle of childish laughter. The chatter of happy adults. The smells of summer. Flowers. Sunkissed skin. Fresh sweat. Barbeques. Warm tarmac. Mud and soil. The coppery aroma of summer rain.

Shaun had gone over these memories a hundred times, a thousand times. So often that the visions became tatty around the edges, like worn photographs. He jumbled through them with abandon, until — even in the saltwater — the tears burned his eyes.

He would never leave; *never*. This was his world, his home, *his life*. This was where he belonged, where he had been happy, where he *would* be happy, he would stay, he would stay, he would stay. And even if they sent someone down here to take him back up, he would fight them off. This was what his soul yearned for; his heart was a dropped anchor that weighed him to the depths of the ocean. He felt its pull, helpless to resist, he would never go back, *never*, and he knew it was all a lie.

The low air alarm buzzed in the silence. It unleashed a cacophony of bubbles before his eyes.

His heart sank with the cold reality of adulthood. The sensation reminded him when the summer holidays drew to an end. The knowledge that school would start soon.

He would go back. He would return. Shaun knew not whether he would Go Down again, once he returned to the surface. These memories — warm, soft, cosy and comforting — were just that. Memories. Gone. Gone. *Gone.* It was safe here, protected here, inside the shell of a clam — and Shaun was the pearl. But that wasn't life. Life was the opposite of that. Life was *up there*, swimming with the sharks. Life was cold, and scary and *exhilarating*. Life was swimming with your shoal, shining and shimmering with bright, hyperactive life. Friends, family, loved ones, enemies, strangers. All swarming around, crossing paths. Bumping into each other, leaving each other, sometimes meeting again, sometimes not.

Down here was the comfort, but down here was also the

decay. The rot. Shaun knew it would suffocate him. Not at first, but over time — seaweed wrapped around the throat of a gull. It would be okay to dip a toe here and there in the pool of nostalgia, but it was a lifeless pool; a pool of things long past. It was not a place meant for living creatures.

And now Shaun understood. He understood his mother, asking him if he *had to Go Down.* He understood his father, asking him if he wanted company. He understood his sister — wise beyond her years — when she said *it was all gone now.* He understood. He understood.

* * *

The Lifeline dangled and floated, more or less where Shaun had left it.

He reattached himself to the cable. Were they in a panic up there? Did they wonder where he was? Did they worry if he was still alive? A *click!* and a *whoosh!* as his regulator took the air from the Lifeline instead of the depleted tank.

Shaun took an extra-deep breath before he double tapped the 'UP' button. And then it pulled him up, from the drowned street. He flew, rose, soared. Up above the city that had been. It was still a city — full of life — but a city no longer meant for mankind.

Shaun shone his Light Cannon around. Not too far away, three silhouettes flew between the skyscrapers. Two whales and their calf. He thought he could hear their melancholy love song as it drifted along with the ocean currents.

The light changed. The blue of the waters intensified. Shaun flicked the Cannon off and, after a moment's hesitation, switched off the Aqualite as well. If the stranger from the

159

darkness wanted to greet him once more, Shaun would not deter them.

He looked up, to catch a glimpse of the ledge from which he had commenced his dive. Shaun could not make out the top of the cliff yet. But he did see the sunlight's fractured beams as they scattered through the waves far above. All around him danced a rainbow of glitter; a beauty from above he had never seen before. Or had never paid attention to.

Shaun rose upwards, from the darkness.

Timebomb

Now

There were too many to fight.

They outnumbered him by 10,000. He watched as they all raced towards him, vengeance in their eyes and murder on their lips. They came in a mob and clamoured for his blood. Each wanted to say, "I helped kill him. I was part of it."

He stood still. He didn't flinch and he didn't recoil. His hand brushed against the thing in his pocket, and his fingers clutched at it; ready, *waiting*.

The throng thundered down on him, oblivious to what was to come. He grinned. Even after it was over, they still wouldn't understand. They'd trample the ground into dust, confusion written across their faces. Their unsatiated blood lust would drive them mad.

He could do it now, of course. But where would the fun be in that? Where would the *showmanship* be? No, best to wait until the last possible moment. To delay the act until they were *about to get him*, and then...

Of course, Dara wouldn't have done such a thing. She would

have completed the mission and then gotten out of there in the blink of an eye. Nothing more than a breeze that lifts the curtains. Silent like a breath, swift like the fall of a raindrop. She wouldn't have even *used* it. And would likely tell *him* off for it — a "waste of precious resources". Dara would have only employed it in an absolute emergency.

But Raiden *wanted* to use it. Why have it and not use it? It would be like being a millionaire but unable to spend money. He didn't *need* to use it, *oh no*. He was good at his job, and he knew it. If his actions had necessitated the use of the thing, he wouldn't have come so recommended at all.

But, as it was, Raiden was at the top of his field.

Well, *almost.*

* * *

Then

"Oh no." She shook her head. "No. *No.*"

"But, Dara, he's the best—"

"*Excuse me?*"

"Well, *second best—*"

"Hang on, a second," said Raiden.

"Look, I'm just saying—"

"I said, *no*," said Dara. She folded her arms across her chest. "Am I not the captain of this crew?"

"Well, *yes*, but—"

"But?"

"Ah, maybe we oughta forget it." Raiden turned to walk away.

"*Wait!*" Franky grabbed him by the shoulder. "Please. Wait?"

Raiden nodded. "Sure. But don't ever touch me like that again, you hear?"

"Don't threaten *my* crew, you—" The word that came from her mouth made both men wince.

"Wait. Just… *wait*," said Franky. He stood in the middle of them, hands raised in case either one of them decided to go for the other. "Dara, he *is* very good. You know that."

"I'm the *best*." Raiden folded his arms and rolled his eyes.

Franky ignored him. "He comes with a certain… *reputation—*"

"Yeah, I'll say," said Dara. She snorted and turned away with a childish glare.

"Look, guys, I know you don't like each other, but—"

"Ya think?" Raiden and Dara said in unison, with the same sarcastic inflexion. Looks of horror flashed across their faces and they both turned away in disgust.

"*Look. Guys,*" said Franky through gritted teeth. "I *know* you don't like each other, but we don't have a choice."

"There's *always* a choice Franky, didn't I teach you *anything?*" said Dara.

"Yeah, Franky…" mocked Raiden.

"Oh my *God*, you two are the absolute *worst*, do you know that?" Franky turned to his captain and pointed at her leg, which was in a cast and on a raised cushion. "Do you honestly think you can pull off a mission with your leg like *that?*"

"Can do it better than *him*." She pointed to Raiden with her chin.

"*Really*, Dara? *Really?*"

She squinted at him, and her eyes shot daggers, but she said nothing.

"And *you*." Franky turned to Raiden. "I know how broke

you are. You think that debt collectors don't *talk?* I know for a *fact* there are three scumbag moneylenders out there that want your head on a platter!"

Raiden paled as the colour drained from his face. Dara started to laugh, but Franky shot her a glare that told her she shouldn't. "You both need each other. And don't you dare argue with me." He looked from one to the other. He challenged them to say something to the contrary. "And, perhaps most importantly, *I* need both of you. I can't make ends meet if we can't take any jobs, Dara… and he's the best out there. We both know he is. Hell, *he* knows he is, the cocky sonofa—"

"*Hey!*"

"Sorry."

"It's true."

An awkward silence fell upon the room. Franky lowered his hands. "So, do we have an understanding?"

Dara and Raiden glared at each other, and then flicked their eyes back to Franky.

"Fine," mumbled Dara.

"Fine," said Raiden.

"*Great!*" Franky sounded more enthusiastic than he felt. "Well, done, guys. I really think that you've—"

"Yeah, yeah, let's talk shop," said Raiden. He shushed him.

"Agreed. Let's get on with it. Shut up, Franky."

"I—" started Franky. He looked from Dara to Raiden but then he gave up and sighed. He deflated. "Oh, fine."

"Okay, so, let's go over the plan…" Dara clicked a button and brought up a holographic map.

It hovered in the centre of the room.

* * *

164

Now

Raiden pulled the object out of his pocket with the flourish of a well-practised magician.

He saw the look of urgency in the eyes of those nearest to him as they sprinted towards his location. The gleam of fear that flashed across their faces. They *knew* he was about to pull something off, like a rabbit out of a hat. They just didn't know *what*.

The natives of Raghajiv bent their heads low and *threw themselves* into their sprint.

To catch the blasphemous thief.

* * *

Then

"They want *what?*" asked Raiden, astounded. "Are they *crazy?*"

"Yes. Crazy *rich*," said Dara. "What's the matter, is it too big of a job for—" she adopted a babylike voice "—the great Raiden?"

"No, of course not! It's just… this is gonna upset a lot of people, you do realise?"

"*Obviously.*" She rolled her eyes. "That's why they're hiring a crew to do it for them. If it was an easy task, they'd do it themselves, wouldn't they? Besides, the added danger means they're adding a few more zeroes to our paycheck, which is always appreciated."

"How much are they paying?"

"That's for me to know, Raiden. You'll get your previously

discussed share, as agreed. Now, let's talk *details…*"

* * *

Now

Raiden rolled the glass orb in his palm.

The object was delicate and prone to shattering — its makers had designed it so. When the outer shell cracked, it would spill its contents across the ground.

And into the atmosphere.

He watched the horde close in on him like a wildfire. The moment drew nearer. *Almost there*, he told himself. *Almost… almost… Three, two, one and—*

Raiden smashed the orb onto the floor at his feet.

* * *

Then

"Any idea why they want it?"

Dara shrugged. "None of my concern. As long as they pay up, they can smash it for all I care. Let 'em chop it up and eat it. Let them deface it. I don't care."

"But, it's a religious symbol," said Raiden. He trod with caution.

"Oh, *what?* What happened in those years that we stopped working together, Raiden? You didn't suddenly see the light, did you? You haven't gone all wacko on me, have you?"

"Hey, no. I'm not… a *believer*," he said. He took care with the word. "But I wouldn't talk about the followers like that. I mean, who knows? Right? I mean—"

"Do you want the job or not, man? You might be the best, but there's a thousand others out there who are good enough who'd do the job without asking this many questions. Plenty of people need the cash."

"Whoa, *whoa*, Dara. Of course, I want the job!"

"Then stop talking as if you don't."

* * *

Now

It felt as if all the air vanished from the surface of the planet.

Before the glass had tinkled to the ground, an aqua blue bubble bloomed from the container. It blossomed outwards and encapsulated him. For a second it stayed there and hovered around him. It crackled with electric life. Psychedelic patterns swirled into infinity across its surface.

And then it erupted outwards. It rocketed into the oncoming horde.

A subsonic *BOOM* rattled Raiden's eardrums and all the hairs on his body stood on end. His lungs had the breath pulled from them, and he uttered a shocked little, "Oof!" Raiden felt like someone had hit him in the gut and winded him.

A moment later, he roared with laughter.

The mob was still there — nobody harmed. But they moved in slow motion towards him as their skins crackled with blue lightning. Somewhere in the crowd, someone continued to shout. "Geeeeeeeettttt hiiiiiiiiimmmm!" The voice was deep. And hilarious.

He giggled like a schoolchild and stepped out into the throng, backpack heavy on his shoulders. The thing was right there within grabbing distance — the understanding was in their eyes. But they couldn't get it. He laughed again. This was brilliant. Raiden waltzed through the crowd. He took special attention to lock eyes with as many murderous gazes as he could. Every single one of them would slaughter him in an instant if they had the chance. And here he was, right within their grasp. And they were, for all intents and purposes, statues.

Raiden pranced and bounced around them. It was as if they danced in zero gravity. Or tried to wade through a lake of treacle. His laughter tinkled through the air like falling glass. *Fantastic*, he thought. *This is utterly fantastic!*

He knew he should make his hasty getaway. But Raiden jumped and skipped through the pack of would-be assailants for the next 20 minutes.

He laughed all the while.

* * *

Then

"So, how will we deliver it? I assume people will be looking for it."

"You assume correctly, Mr Genius. We're gonna have the handoff on Tartrak."

"Tartrak? Dara, are you sure about this?"

"I know what I'm doing. And whilst I'm captain, you won't

question me. Just do your job, Raiden."

"Well, *okay…*"

* * *

Now

The ship was on the beach, the rear ramp lowered onto the sand.

Franky waited outside. He leaned against the ship, arms crossed. He looked annoyed. "What took you?"

"Nothing." Raiden stifled a giggle.

"Did something go wrong?"

"No, nothing at all. Went off without a hitch."

Franky sized him up. "I hope you're telling the truth. For your sake. Dara's *pissed*. Did you get it?"

Raiden patted his heavy backpack. "Right here."

Franky nodded, then scanned the horizon. "Nobody saw you?"

Raiden grinned. "Like I said. It went off without a hitch." He avoided the truth, but it wasn't a lie. At least, not in his own eyes.

"All right. Climb in the back. We're leaving Raghajiv right now. Heading to meet the buyers."

"Is Dara…?"

Franky nodded. "Yep. Good luck."

And with that, Franky climbed into the cockpit and started the ship's engines.

* * *

Then

"Geahek? *Geahek?* Dara, I—"

"Stop. I said to not question my authority."

"I know, but, Geahek is a mean… *whatever* he is. And his gang? Dara, they're wanted dead or alive on every major planet."

"You think I don't know that?" Dara hissed. "But he's paying *big bucks*. Don't you get it? If we prove we can handle Geahek without wetting our pants, the rest of the clients will just fall into place. The *infamy*."

"I—" started Raiden, but then he gave up. He shook his head and sighed.

There was little use in arguing with Dara. He'd learnt that many moons ago.

Once she had an idea in her head…

* * *

Now

Dara hadn't been as angry with him as he'd anticipated.

She was happy he had the idol. She held the thing in her hands and rotated it around to get a proper look at it. "Over 3,000 years old…" she said, in slight awe. "I mean, I know it's got massive importance, but it *is* only made from bronze. It's not like it's gold or crystal or whatever."

"Dara…" Raiden looked at her as if she had two heads. "This idol is one of the central pillars of the entire Raghajiv *religion*. You are holding something that people have killed for and died for. Something that people *believe in*, something people *pray* to. There are thousands of people out there that think that when they die, they meet—" he gestured towards the statue.

"Wow," said Dara "That was quite a speech." She jabbed the idol in his direction. "You should get into politics, y'know."

Before Raiden could retort, the pilot interrupted them. "We're here," said Franky, from upfront.

Through the windshield, they saw the icy wastes of Tartrak, the dead planet.

* * *

Then

"It's not too late to turn the job down, you know," he told her on the ride to Raghajiv. "You can still—"

"Turn Geahek *down?*"

Raiden turned the thought over in his mind. "Nope. You're right. That would get us killed. If you told Geahek you'd do it, we better do it, hm?"

* * *

Now

And now, here they were on their knees in the snow, hands behind their heads, guns trained on them.

Raiden wanted to say 'I told you so'. *No, probably shouldn't*, he thought. He looked out the corner of his eye and caught

Dara's attention. "Told you so," he whispered.

"Tiihuh," she whispered through gritted teeth.

"Hm?"

"Tiihuh," she repeated, jaw clenched.

"*What?*"

"Hnh hn tiihuh."

"Oh, for goodness sake, will you just *say* whatever it is you're trying to say?"

"I said, *throw the timebomb!*"

Raiden's words caught in his throat.

"Throw it, Raiden!" shouted Dara. Her eyes urged. Around them, Geahek's guards shouted and bellowed orders.

"I, uh… I don't have it."

"*What?*"

"I don't… I don't have it. I might have, ah, used it back on Raghajiv."

The guards swarmed around them. A blur of black armour against the icy blueish whites of Tartrak's wastelands.

"You *what?* You blithering idiot! You utter moron! You—"

And that was when one of Geahek's guards struck him on the back of the head and he blacked out.

* * *

Then

"I wonder what he wants it for," pondered Raiden out loud. "Why chase down an ancient religious idol?"

"Who cares, as long as we get paid?" replied Dara. "And don't go off about the—" she did mock air-quotes "—*significance of such an artefact.* Let's just do the work, get paid, and then go our separate ways. 'Cause your face is already annoying me."

"Your voice, too," added Franky.

Dara nodded. "Yeah, and your voice."

* * *

Now

"Lucky for you, we get to spend a lot more time together," he said. He offered her a chirpy smile. "Silver linings, and all that, huh?"

"For God's sake, Raiden, *shut up.*"

"Yeah, Raiden, shut it," growled Franky.

In the room beyond, someone tutted. Geahek stepped from the shadows. "So much infighting, it's a wonder you lot were able to pull off the heist at all." He bounced the idol in his hand.

"Why don't you hurry up and kill us already?" snapped Dara. "Stop toying with us!" As the words tumbled out of her mouth, Raiden knew she hadn't figured it out yet. There were the objects on their legs, for a start.

"Kill you?" Geahek asked. "Why on earth would I *kill you?* You're the best heist crew I've ever had!" His boyish grin bordered on the maniacal. "No, no. I'm not going to *kill* you, gosh *no.* In fact, what I propose is an… *opportunity.*"

"Oh, here we go," mumbled Raiden. He fiddled with the ankle monitor strapped to his leg. It flashed an intermittent red light.

A look of unadulterated rage flashed across Geahek's face. But he maintained composure. "I propose you continue working for me. And when I say 'work', I do *not* mean that you will be getting paid." His eyes crawled over Raiden. "And please stop playing with that. It's not a toy, and you won't get it off." Geahek's voice dropped down a register: "Believe me."

"What kinda work?" asked Dara.

"Well…" He scrutinised the idol. "This wasn't the only religious artefact I am after. And you weren't the only crew I hired. The problem is that the others… they, ah, suffered casualties. In fact, you are the only crew that returned alive."

"Oh…"

"I want you to go and retrieve the other artefacts."

"Which others?" asked Raiden. An awful feeling rose in his chest.

"I think you know," said Geahek with a wicked grin. "But here's a hint for job number one: *Quowiduw*." The exotic word rolled off his tongue.

Raiden closed his eyes and swore.

Dara looked confused. "What? *What?*"

"I'll leave you to… *discuss* the proposition," said Geahek. He ignored her. "Of course, it's either 'yes' or it's death, you must realise. Anywho…" He swaggered through the doors and whistled a jaunty tune.

"What did he say?" Dara turned in her narrow cage.

Raiden sighed. "Basically, we either get killed by his cronies… *or*, we get killed by religious nuts. Or by mother nature." He looked from Franky to Dara, in the cramped confines of their prisons. "Guys… we're going to Muxel."

Franky and Dara swore in unison.

A Word From the Author

Thank you for reading my second collection of short stories!

If you enjoyed *Under Blankets, Under Stars*, it would mean the world to me if you left a review. Authors such as myself need reviews to gain more exposure. Comments on Amazon, Goodreads, and social media can help spread the word.

But, hey, there's no pressure! You don't have to do anything, I won't be offended. The most important thing is that you enjoyed our time together. I hope some of these stories will stay with you, the way some of my favourite works continue to haunt me. In the best way possible, of course!

Stay safe, and look after one another. There can never be too much love in the world.

All the best,
Josh

Prompt Acknowledgements

ALL HAL'S EVE

Written for the Reedsy prompt: "Write about someone taking a child trick-or-treating for the very first time." — 30th October 2020

* * *

A LITTLE BIT OFF

This story was shortlisted for Reedsy's Weekly Writing Contest: "Write about a person who collects superhero comics." — 3rd July 2020

* * *

A SMALL DEATH

Written for the #BlogBattle prompt: "Miniature" — 10th November 2020

* * *

ASTRO NAUGHT

This story won Reedsy's Weekly Writing Contest: "Write a story about an adventure in space." — 26th September 2019

* * *

BRIDGEMOSS GUARDIANS

This story won Reedsy's Weekly Writing Contest: "Start your story with two characters deciding to spend the night in a graveyard." — 27th October 2020

* * *

BUY ANOTHER BIRTHDAY

Written for the Reedsy prompt: "Write a story that starts with someone returning from a trip." — 4th June 2020

* * *

DON'T PANIC IF I CATCH FIRE

Written for the Reedsy prompt: "Write about someone who is given a bird for the holidays but doesn't know how to take care of it." — 21st December 2020

* * *

DONUM EX DEO

Written for the Reedsy prompt: "Write a story about a character who's too polite to tell someone they don't like a gift given to them." — 20th March 2020

* * *

EARTH.EXE

Written for the #BlogBattle prompt: "Blank" — 4th January

2021

* * *

FEEL LIKE BAKING LOVE

Written for the Reedsy prompt: "Write about two people who run rival bakeries, but fall in love during their town's annual holiday festival." — 8th December 2020

* * *

GEORGE, JENNY, AND THE STARS

Written for the Reedsy prompt: "While cleaning out your attic, you reach into the pocket of a long-forgotten coat and discover an old ticket stub." — 1st February 2019

* * *

HONESTY IN G# MINOR

This story was shortlisted for Reedsy's Weekly Writing Contest: "Write about something you consider yourself an expert in, but do it from the perspective of a total novice." — 15th November 2019

* * *

HOW TO BUILD A BOAT

Written for the Reedsy prompt: "Write a story about someone who finds life meaning in an unexpected place." — 2nd September 2019

* * *

MALEDICTIONS AND MUFFINS

"Written for the Reedsy prompt: Write about someone who works an average job — but incorporate elements of magic into it." — 12th March 2020

* * *

NIGHT TRAIN TO PINEA

Written for the Reedsy prompt: "Write a short story that takes place on a train." — 7th February 2020

* * *

RETURNING THE FAVOUR

Written for the Reedsy prompt: "Two strangers meet at a New Year's Eve party. They spend the party together, and then never see each other again." — 4th January 2020

* * *

ROUTINE

Written for the Reedsy prompt: "Write a story about two best friends." — 21st February 2020

* * *

SEA THE MOON

This story was shortlisted for Reedsy's Weekly Writing Contest: "Write a story in which the lines between awake and dreaming are blurred." — 24th February 2020

* * *

SNOITSEUQ AND SREWSNA

Written for the Reedsy prompt: "Write a story that ends with a character asking a question." — 22nd May 2020

* * *

THE LONELY EARTH

Written for the Reedsy prompt: "Write a story about a person waiting for an answer to a question." — 6th July 2020

* * *

THE THINGS THAT DO NOT FLOAT

This story won Reedsy's Weekly Writing Contest: "Write a story about a teenager visiting the place where they grew up." — 23rd August 2019

* * *

TIMEBOMB

Written for the Reedsy prompt: "Your fingers tensed around the object in your pocket, ready to pull it out at a moment's notice." — 5th December 2019

About the Author

Joshua G. J. Insole is a British writer who lives in the Austrian Alps. His favoured genres are horror and science fiction. Joshua — three-time winner of the Reedsy contest and author of several other shortlisted stories — published his first book, *A Chance of Rain*, in July 2020.

You can connect with me on:
- 🌐 https://joshuainsole.com
- 🐦 https://twitter.com/joshuainsole
- 📘 https://www.facebook.com/JoshuaGJInsole

Also by Joshua G. J. Insole

A Chance of Rain

Over 40 tales of monsters, magic, mystery, and madness. From the real to the weird, from the traumatic to the hilarious. Includes three shortlisted works.

Zeitfracht Medien GmbH
Ferdinand-Jühlke-Straße 7
99095 Erfurt, Deutschland
produktsicherheit@kolibri360.de